Pretty Madcap Dorothy
Or, How She Won a Lover

Laura Jean Libbey

Alpha Editions

This edition published in 2024

ISBN 9789362091239

Design and Setting By

Alpha Editions
www.alphaedis.com

Email - info@alphaedis.com

As per information held with us this book is in Public Domain.
This book is a reproduction of an important historical work.
Alpha Editions uses the best technology to reproduce historical work
in the same manner it was first published to preserve its original nature.
Any marks or number seen are left intentionally to preserve.

Contents

CHAPTER I. ....- 1 -

CHAPTER II. ....- 6 -

CHAPTER III. ....- 12 -

CHAPTER IV. ....- 20 -

CHAPTER V. ....- 25 -

CHAPTER VI. ....- 30 -

CHAPTER VII. ....- 36 -

CHAPTER VIII. ....- 41 -

CHAPTER IX. ....- 46 -

CHAPTER X. ....- 51 -

CHAPTER XI. ....- 56 -

CHAPTER XII. ....- 61 -

CHAPTER XIII. ....- 66 -

CHAPTER XIV. ....- 71 -

CHAPTER XV. ....- 76 -

CHAPTER XVI. ....- 81 -

CHAPTER XVII. ....- 86 -

CHAPTER XVIII. ....- 91 -

CHAPTER XIX. ....- 96 -

CHAPTER XX.	- 101 -
CHAPTER XXI.	- 106 -
CHAPTER XXII.	- 111 -
CHAPTER XXIII.	- 115 -
CHAPTER XXIV.	- 119 -
CHAPTER XXV.	- 123 -
CHAPTER XXVI.	- 127 -
CHAPTER XXVII.	- 132 -
CHAPTER XXVIII.	- 137 -
CHAPTER XXIX.	- 141 -
CHAPTER XXX.	- 146 -
CHAPTER XXXI.	- 150 -
CHAPTER XXXII.	- 154 -
CHAPTER XXXIII.	- 158 -
CHAPTER XXXIV.	- 162 -
CHAPTER XXXV.	- 166 -
CHAPTER XXXVI.	- 171 -
CHAPTER XXXVII.	- 175 -
CHAPTER XXXVIII.	- 178 -
CHAPTER XXXIX.	- 182 -

CHAPTER I.

"It's so hard for working-girls to get acquainted. They never meet a rich young man, and they don't want a poor one. It seems to me that a girl who has to commence early to work for her living might just as well give up forever all hopes of a lover and of marrying," declared Nadine Holt, one of the prettiest girls in the immense book-bindery, to the group of companions who were gathered about her. "It's get up at daylight, swallow your breakfast, and hurry to work; and it's dark before you are out on the street again. How can we ever expect to meet a marriageable fellow?"

"Do you know what *I* think, girls?" cried a shrill but very sweet young voice, from the direction of the window-ledge, adding breathlessly: "I believe if fate has any lover in store for a girl, that he will be sure to just happen to come where she is, on one mission or another. That's the way that it all happens in novels, I took particular pains to notice. These people who write must know just how it is, I reckon."

"Well, now, who would ever have imagined that a chit of a thing like *you*, Dorothy Glenn, would have the impudence to put in your oar, or that you ever thought of lovers, or marrying, and you only sixteen a day or so ago?" cried one. "It's absurd!"

"I wasn't saying anything about *my* ever marrying, I was just telling you what I thought about ever meeting the fellow who is intended for you—'*the* right *one*'—as you call it."

"What if you were in a desert?" suggested Nadine, with a curl of her red lip. "Surely you couldn't expect a young man would ever find a business that would bring him out there to you, could you?"

"Why not?" cried pretty little Dorothy. "Of course fate would send my Prince Charming even into a desert to find me," cooed Dorothy. "And as to the business that would bring him—why, he could come there to capture the ostriches which are to be found only in the heart of the desert—so there! You know the old adage: 'People meet where hills and mountains don't.' I tell you there's some truth in that."

"It's a good thing to have so much assurance and hope," said Nadine, with a curl of her lip. "I trust that you may find plenty of lovers in the future, though I doubt it."

"I have plenty now," declared Dorothy, waltzing nimbly about the floor, as only a bright, happy, thoughtless young girl can who is free from care. "I couldn't count all who make eyes at me now, so what will it be when I get as old as the rest of you girls?"—this a trifle maliciously, for every one of them was at least twenty, and that seemed rather *passée* to this bit of femininity of sweet sixteen.

Some one noticed that the huge clock on the mantel wanted just three minutes to one, so the fragments of luncheon were crammed back into their baskets, and the girls, chatting and laughing, went back to their work, for they had a very particular foreman. But one of their number, Jessie Staples, hung back to have a word with Dorothy.

"I hope that you will not grow into a flirt," she said, slipping her arm about Dorothy's waist and looking into the young girl's flushed face with serious eyes, adding: "This brings me to the question that I intended asking you this noon. Where did you meet that young car conductor who walked up as far as your home with you last night? Do tell me, little Dorothy."

"Were you spying upon me, you mean thing?" cried Dorothy Glenn, blushing as fiery red as the crimson heart of a peony, and stamping angrily the tiniest of little feet; and she flung her companion's arm from her as though it had stung her.

"Can't you tell me?" pleaded Jessie, earnestly. "Remember, you have no one to warn you. You are an orphan in this great, cold world, and—and you are so young that you don't know life, and can not realize that every young man who smiles into your eyes and says flattering things is *not* in love. When you have no relative to confide in, you ought to have a girl friend older and wiser than yourself. Let me be that friend to you, Dorothy."

As she listened, the momentary anger died out of the girl's face. She couldn't keep angry with anybody very long, and quite before Jessie had finished her sentence a pair of plump white arms were thrown round her neck and Dorothy's soft, peachy pink cheek was nestling against her own, while the sweet young voice whispered:

"Won't you breathe it, Jess, if I tell you the greatest secret in the whole wide world? Promise on your word and honor that you won't and I'll tell you, and it will fairly make you hold your breath. It's just like those grand love stories all of us girls like to crowd around together at lunch hour and read in the Fireside Companion, when we pick up the special copies they throw around; only this is in real life, you know."

"I promise," returned Jessie Staples, gravely; "only I hope this isn't a ruse to turn off the question about the young car conductor whom I saw you with."

"Oh, no! the secret is about him," laughed Dorothy, gleefully, "and it will make you open your eyes wider than they are now when you hear it; and it's so dreadfully romantic, too. You know how Nadine Holt has been boasting of late about the handsome new conductor on the Broadway car, on whom she has 'made a mash,' as she phrases it. Well, the young man you saw me talking to—is he."

"What?" gasped Jessie. "Do you mean it was Nadine's beau to whom you were talking?"

"He's *not* her beau!" declared Dorothy, flushing up redly and angrily. "He doesn't care a snap of his finger for Nadine. He told me so."

"He—told—you—so?" repeated Jessie Staples, too amazed at the instant to frame any other remark, while the thought flashed through her brain how deeply Nadine Holt loved this handsome young man, and that she was confident of a proposal of marriage from him sooner or later. She had often told Jessie as much as that of late.

"It was only last week that I first met him," Dorothy went on, "and it happened in this way: I came down, just by chance, on his car, and—and I noticed that he looked at me rather admiringly, as he changed my fifty-cent piece, while standing beside me; and—and I noticed, too, that he leaned against me a little more than the occasion demanded, or at least I fancied so; but perhaps it was the jolting of the car. I took little shy peeps at him. I wanted to see what he looked like, Nadine had been sounding his praises so. I found he was dreadfully nice, quite the handsomest young fellow I had ever seen—elegantly formed, straight as an arrow, with such a beautiful dark mustache, dark hair, and laughing black eyes, and the whitest of white hands. When he helped me off the car he held my hand so tightly and so long that I felt terribly embarrassed and did not know what to do or say. But, oh! he was *so* polite! I dropped my eyes and never looked at him as I stepped off. How I ever got into the other car I never knew. A moment later the other conductor came around for my fare, and then—oh, horrors! I could not find my pocket-book. I searched frantically in every pocket. 'I—I must have *lost* my purse,' I faltered, beginning to cry, for I saw he did not believe me, and thought that I meant to beat my way, as they call it, when just at that instant puffing and panting, up came the other conductor—the handsome fellow whom I had just left.

"'You dropped your purse on the seat of my car,' he said, raising his hat from his dark curls. 'Permit me to return it to you.'

"I was so overjoyed to get it that I forgot to thank him. I remembered later that I had not done so. And what do you think? that very evening he called with a book I had also left on the seat, and which I had entirely forgotten.

My name and address were written on the fly-leaf. Just at that moment one of the young men from the book-bindery happened along who knew him, and he introduced us. I did not invite him in, but we stood and talked for an hour or more on the steps, and he asked at length for the pleasure of my company to go with him to the theater the following evening, if my folks were willing.

"I told him I had no relatives to consult, and that I'd like ever so much to go, but—but I had heard that he was Nadine Holt's regular company. Oh, Jess, how angry he got when I said that! He flushed to the very roots of his dark hair. You ought to have seen him.

"'Pardon me, but I am *not*!' he replied, 'though I hear that she is circulating such a story; but there is no better authority on the subject than myself. I have spoken to her a few times; but it is ridiculous for a girl to presume, if a man is pleasant to her, that he wants to marry her. I cannot even say that I admire Miss Nadine Holt. As a rule a man like myself does not admire a girl whose acquaintance he can form through a handkerchief flirtation.

"I thought of telling Nadine that, but you know what a fury she is. Why, she would almost kill me, I believe, if she once got an inkling that I knew about it.

"Well, to make a long story short, it so chanced that he happened along our street every night after that, and always found me, quite by chance, sitting out on the steps, and so he stopped for a chat. And now comes the most wonderful part of the affair. He is no *real* street-car conductor at all. I don't mean just that, but—oh, Jess! this is what I mean: he—he bet with a number of young gentlemen the last election and lost the wager. If he lost he was to come to New York and be a street-car conductor for three months, and that is what he did. He is a young lawyer in a small town near here, and has great expectations, he says.

"His time will be up to-morrow, Jessie, and then he is going back to his home, and—and I shall never see him again. He is like a prince in disguise—such as we read about. I always thought him too grand and polite to be only a street-car conductor."

Jessie Staples felt greatly relieved in her heart that he was going away so soon, but she was too wise to say so to Dorothy, knowing that if one attempts to break up an infatuation on the part of a girl of that age, ten to one it makes matters only worse.

"Life will never be the same to me after Harry Langdon goes, for, Jessie, I—I have learned to care for him. I couldn't help myself though I tried hard not to, and to be gay and jolly before all the girls. But, oh, Jessie, pity me! My heart is breaking! I wish I could die!"

They did not notice, as they moved on, that the door near where they had stood talking was partly ajar, nor did they see the girl who had paused in the entry outside almost at the very beginning of their conversation. It was Nadine Holt, and she had heard every word, from beginning to end, that Dorothy had uttered; and even after they had passed on she stood there, cold and motionless as a statue cut in marble.

"Great God in heaven! this explains Harry Langdon's sudden coolness," she muttered, with a great, choking sob; "but if Dorothy Glenn attempts to take my lover from me—let her beware! this earth will not be broad enough to hold the two of us. It will be war to the very death between us, and we shall see which one of us shall win him!"

By a violent effort Nadine controlled her wild grief and passed into the work-room. It was only her indomitable pride that kept her from taking her hat and sacque and going straight home and to her bed, there to weep her very heart out—aye, weep her very life out, if she could. If her lover was fickle, Nadine told herself that she did not care to live and face the dull, cold world, for what is life and the world to a young girl if the lover on whom she has set her heart and her hopes proves false to her?

Chapter II.

From the moment that Nadine Holt heard the story of the perfidy of her lover she was a changed being.

She went wearily enough to the lodging-house she called home, and paced the floor up and down the live-long night.

"He was pleased enough with me before Dorothy Glenn's pink-and-white baby face came between us," she moaned, clinching her hands tightly together and bursting ever and anon into a flood of tears.

She looked around at the little, stuffy room, and thought of all her girlish day-dreams—of the sweet hopes she had had of soon leaving those dingy four walls, and of having a little bower of a cottage to call "home," with a handsome young husband all her own to love her.

She had pictured every scene to herself—just how each cozy room should be furnished, and what vines and flowers should grow in the garden, and the pretty dresses she would wear, and how she would stand at the window and watch for handsome Harry to come home each night, and what a dear, cozy life they would lead, loving each other so dearly.

And now what of those vanished day-dreams? Ah! God in heaven pity her! they lay in ruins around her, and heart-wrecked, heart-broken, she was facing the cold, bleak world again.

It had been by the greatest effort that she had looked in Dorothy's face during the day that followed without betraying her bitter hatred of her; but as the hours crept on, and she saw Dorothy's glance wander uneasily now and then toward the clock, her intense rage grew almost uncontrollable.

"She is longing for the hours to pass, so that she may join *him*," thought Nadine, and her black eyes fairly scintillated at the thought.

Suddenly Dorothy raised her curly head from her work.

"Girls!" she exclaimed, shrilly and eagerly, "have you all forgotten that Monday is Labor Day? What are you going to do with yourselves?"

A score or more of voices answered at random that they thought it had been decided long since that they were all going up the Hudson on an excursion.

"I can't go on the excursion with you, girls," returned Dorothy, "for I've got another engagement."

"Bring your company with you," chorused a dozen or more of the girls.

Dorothy glanced up hastily and met Nadine's burning eyes fixed intently upon her.

She started, turned deathly pale, and then turned defiantly away, wondering if Nadine could by any means suspect that the engagement she had was to accompany handsome Harry Langdon to the matinée.

She wondered vaguely if Jessie, to whom she had confided this, had betrayed her.

The look in Nadine Holt's eyes as they met her own startled her.

The bell which released the girls from the work-room that night had scarcely rung ere Dorothy had on her sacque and sailor hat and was fairly flying down the steps and out into the street.

"I hope to goodness that I shall escape Jack to-night!" she muttered. "He can not get out as soon as I do, and I will be almost home while he is waiting for me at the bottom of the stairs;" and a little, light, airy laugh bubbled from her red lips.

Jack, as she called him, was one of the gilders in the book-bindery—a tall, handsome, manly young fellow of four-and-twenty, whose only failing was that he loved little Dorothy Glenn to distraction.

"Yes, I shall escape Jack, sure, to-night!" laughed Dorothy again.

But the laugh died from her lips, for at that instant there was the sound of hurried footsteps behind her—footsteps she knew but too well—and the next instant Jack Garner stood beside her.

"Dorothy!" he panted, "Why didn't you wait for me, little girl?"

Dorothy started guiltily.

"Why, gracious! is it you, Jack?" she cried. "I certainly thought you had gone home long ago, and so I hurried away."

His handsome face brightened; the dark shadow was quickly dispelled from his earnest, brown eyes.

"Do you know, Dorothy," he said, "I was half afraid that you had run away from me intentionally; and yet I could hardly bring myself to believe it, the thought gave me such a sharp pang of pain at the heart." The girl laughed a little nervously.

"I wanted to talk to you about Labor Day," he said earnestly; "but I fear what I have to say will grieve you, dear." ("Oh, gracious goodness, that's just what I expected!" was the thought that flashed through her guilty little brain.) "Dorothy," he said, huskily, "I'm afraid that I will not be able to get off Labor Day, although it is a legal holiday and I had set my heart upon taking you somewhere. We have found that there is some work which must be got out, or it will mean a heavy loss to our employers. I was the only one whom they felt they could call upon to help them in their dilemma, and I could not refuse them, even though a vision of your pretty, disappointed face rose up before my mind's eye. I knew you would be expecting me to take you somewhere on Labor Day. Oh! Dorothy, how can I make amends for it?"

To his great surprise, she laughed gayly.

"Don't trouble yourself about me, Jack," she exclaimed. "I won't mind it one bit;" and her pink-and-white face fairly dimpled over with smiles.

He opened his brown eyes wide and looked at her in surprise, remembering quite well that for many a week past Dorothy had been looking forward to this holiday and calculating how she should spend it.

"But you will be so disappointed, little one," he reiterated, earnestly, and not a little puzzled by the way she took it.

Again she laughed—a little, light, airy laugh that somehow grated on his nerves.

"I was thinking," he continued, "that perhaps you would like to go somewhere with my cousin Barbara—go up the river, or to a matinée, or some place like that. I would pay all the bills, of course, and—"

"Go with your cousin Barbara?" she cut in. "No, I guess not. It's just like you not to want me to have a good time. If *you* can't be there, Jack Garner, pray excuse me from going with *her*!"

He looked down at her with grieved eyes.

"Barbara is not as young and gay as you are, I know, dear," he said, huskily; "but, oh! if you only knew what a good, gentle soul she is, and how kind her heart is! She would go out of her way—do anything she could to give you a few hours' pleasure, because—because she knows how dear you are to me."

Dorothy shrugged her shoulders and curled her pretty red lips scornfully. Barbara Hallenbeck, his quiet, sedate cousin, was four-and-twenty. No wonder that gay little Dorothy did not consider her quite companionable for a day's outing.

"She would be very glad to take you to the matinée, Dorothy," he persisted. "*Do* consent to go with her, and then I will feel quite happy, for I shall feel sure that you are having a pleasant day, even if I am not with you.

Otherwise, I should be so troubled, thinking of you sitting all alone in the house."

She looked up innocently into his face.

"I need not stay in the house if I do not like," she retorted. "There's a number of girls from the bindery going on an excursion up the river, and they have invited me."

Poor, innocent Jack! it did not occur to him then that, although she had remarked she was invited, she had not said she was going. He jumped at conclusions readily enough.

"I am so glad, Dorothy!" he exclaimed, joyfully. "I know if you are with a crowd of the girls the day will pass pleasantly for you. But you will not forget in the midst of all your happiness to give a thought to me, will you?" he whispered, with a world of tenderness in his voice.

"Of course not," she said, promptly.

"Especially when your eye rests upon our betrothal-ring," he added, wistfully.

Dorothy blushed alarmingly red, then paled as quickly, at the mention of the ring.

The truth may as well be told here and now: Dorothy, like many another silly, thoughtless young girl, had drifted into an engagement with Jack just to get the ring which he wore on his finger, which she had admired with all her heart and longed to possess.

But with Dorothy, possession had dimmed her appreciation for the little turquois and pearl affair which adorned her finger, and at which handsome Harry Langdon had glanced so contemptuously only the evening before, and then down at the elegant monogrammed diamond ring which glistened on his own white, shapely hand.

Only that very day Dorothy had wished with all her heart that she could get up some excuse to break what Jack considered an engagement, and give him back his little cheap pearl and turquois ring; but the occasion did not seem to be quite ripe, and Jack, poor fellow! had been kinder to her than ever that day.

At the corner she hesitated. It would never do to walk much farther with Jack and stand a chance of meeting handsome Harry Langdon, she told herself.

"I have a little shopping to do, and I shall have to leave you here," she said, hastily; and she made her parting very brief with Jack.

He noticed it, and a sudden fear stirred his heart. He looked after the slender figure flitting away through the slanting sunshine, with his soul in his eyes.

"She is so dear to me," he murmured. "I—I often think I would go mad if I were to lose her."

He walked slowly down the street, but, contrary to his usual custom, he did not turn his footsteps homeward, but proceeded aimlessly along the crowded thoroughfare.

How far he went Jack Garner never knew. Suddenly in turning a corner the first object his eyes fell upon was Dorothy, and by her side a tall, handsome dark-eyed young man whose arm was linked with hers, and they were walking along, deeply engaged in conversation, oblivious to the whole world.

He stood quite still; the heart in his bosom seemed to almost tear itself asunder with one mighty throb. Was it Dorothy, or did his eyes deceive him? He quickened his pace until he stood beside them. The impulse was strong within him to seize the girl's hand and tear her from her companion. The blood surged like fire through his veins.

But before he could put his mad thought into execution the crowd on the thronged thoroughfare swept between them.

In that instant Dorothy's companion called a cab and placed the girl in it. The door closed with a bang, and the next instant the vehicle was whirling down the avenue, and turning around the first corner was instantly lost to sight.

Quick as the lightning's flash Jack leaped upon a passing car. He felt intuitively that the stranger was taking Dorothy to her home. This car would pass the door. He would confront them there, even though they had gone by another street.

By a strange fatality he had in his breast pocket a small revolver which a friend had asked him to call for that day at a store where it was being repaired, and bring to him, as Jack would be passing that way. It was an unlucky moment for Jack, Heaven knows, when he consented to call for the fatal revolver for his friend.

As his hand touched it in his breast pocket a terrible thought flashed across his excited brain.

Ten minutes later he reached the cottage where Dorothy boarded. One of the bindery girls was sitting on the porch as he came up.

"Why, hello, Jack!" she cried. "What are you doing here?"

"Where's Dorothy?" he interrupted, quickly. "Is she in the house yet? I want the truth. You must tell me!"

The girl looked in Jack's face, and dared not tell him all.

Chapter III.

Jessie Staples—for it was she—looked at Jack Garner with troubled eyes. She knew how much he cared for Dorothy, and she realized that it would never do to tell him that his fickle sweetheart had gone riding with another man. He was hot-tempered, and in jealousy there is little reason. Like the wise girl that she was, Jessie made excuses for her friend.

"No, Dorothy is not here, Jack," she said, presently; "but I feel sure she would have been had she known you were coming. She has gone to spend the evening with one of the girls, who sent her lover specially to bring Dorothy over, with the request that he was not to come back without her; and no doubt Dorothy will pass Sunday with her."

"Which one of the girls is it?" he inquired.

"I don't really know that," said Jessie, a little faintly.

Jack Garner drew a great, long breath of relief, and the old happy smile lighted up his face in an instant.

What a foolish fellow he had been to mistrust Dorothy! he told himself. But, after all, he was glad he had come and seen Jessie and thus had the horrible doubt removed from his mind.

"Well, it does not matter so much, Jess, that I did not see her. I did not want anything in particular. I am glad she will have a pleasant time this evening and to-morrow. And about your holiday. I suppose you will be going on the excursion with the rest of the girls on Monday?"

"Oh, yes!" replied Jessie lightly but constrainedly.

He drew nearer and looked wistfully into her face.

"I can not go, unfortunately," he said, "but I hope, Jess, that you will see that Dorothy has as good a time as the rest of the girls." He stopped a moment, and looked down confusedly, as if at a loss to know how to proceed with the rest of his sentence, but concluded at length to break right into it boldly. "If I were there I would treat all you girls to as much ice-cream as you could eat," he went on with a laugh. "But, seeing that I am *not* to be one of the party, I want you to do the honors for me, Jess, and here's the money to pay for it, with my compliments to the crowd."

And as he spoke he drew a crisp bill from his vest pocket and thrust it into Jessie's hand.

"Oh, Jack," cried the girl, "you are too good and too kind!" and she felt rather guilty as she took it, for she knew that he was giving it solely that they would make it pleasant for pretty little Dorothy, and she knew that Dorothy was not to be there.

Only that day she had confessed to her that she had made an engagement to go to the matinée with the handsome car conductor.

But there would be a tragedy if Jack got an inkling of this, she well knew. She had deceived him, poor fellow; but was it not for the best, under the circumstances?

Jack went to his home with a light heart, and much relieved in feelings. It was well for him that he did not know just how Dorothy was passing those very moments.

When Harry Langdon had met Dorothy on the street that afternoon he had quite hoped to slip by her unnoticed. Not that he was displeased to see her; but the girl was dressed so cheaply, and, to make matters worse, she carried her little dinner-basket on her arm, and he knew that if any of his friends were to see him they would smile in derision, for they could not help knowing by the dinner-basket that his companion was a working-girl.

His pride was the one fault of his life. He felt that he was quite handsome enough to woo and win an heiress, if one chanced in his way. In fact, that was what he was looking for.

It would never do to be seen walking along the streets with this pretty little working-girl, and it was for this very reason that Langdon had called a cab to take her home.

"The ride is too short," he said, as they reached the cottage where Dorothy lived, and where Jessie Staples was awaiting her on the porch. "Let us go around a few blocks; I want to talk to you about the arrangements for the outing."

Nothing loath, Dorothy consented, and away they whirled down the street; and it was very fortunate too, for in less than three minutes later Jack had appeared at the cottage.

"I have been wondering if you really cared to go to the matinée on Labor Day," said Langdon, in his low, sweet, smooth voice, which had never yet failed to capture the hearts of susceptible young girls. "I was wondering if you would not prefer a sail up the river. I understand that there is to be quite an excursion to West Point."

The truth is Langdon had just discovered that several of his acquaintances were to be at the matinée on that day, and he regretted that he had invited

Dorothy to go, realizing how terribly ashamed he would be of the shabby clothes of the girl whose only recommendation was her pretty young face, and he had determined that he should not take Dorothy to that matinée, at any cost.

"Why, I would just as soon go to the excursion as to the matinée," declared Dorothy; "but there's one objection—all the rest of the girls in the book-bindery are going up on the boat to West Point, and among them Nadine Holt."

Langdon smothered back a fierce imprecation behind his silky curled mustache.

"Then we will abandon the West Point trip." he said, laughingly. "But we can go to Staten Island, besides, I think it will be quite as enjoyable, for, now that I think of it, there will be an immense crowd there. The picnic grounds are to be thrown open to the public, and they are to have a grand garden *fete*, with dancing and so forth."

"Oh, I should enjoy that more than I could tell you!" cried Dorothy, clapping her hands, her blue eyes expanding wide with expectancy. "I adore dancing, and I was never at a garden-party in all my life, and I have read so much about them."

"We can remain all the afternoon and evening, have refreshments, and then come home on the steamer. It will be a beautiful moonlight night, and when the band plays on the deck you will enjoy it hugely, Dorothy."

The girl's eyes sparkled and her cheeks glowed.

Soon afterward the cab stopped before Dorothy's cottage again, and, with a shy, sweet smile, she bade her admirer "good-night," and flitted up the steps and into the hall, and directly into the arms of Jessie Staples, who was awaiting her there.

"Oh, Dorothy!" she began, reproachfully, "how *could* you do it?"

"Do what?" cried Dorothy, with a very innocent air.

"Come riding home from work with that stranger!" cried Jessie, reproachfully.

The gayest laugh that ever was heard broke from Dorothy's ripe red lips, and her blue eyes fairly danced.

"I did not think that *you*, of all other girls, would be jealous, Jessie Staples!" she declared.

"I am not jealous," responded the girl, quietly—"only I pity you for your want of sense in being fascinated by a handsome stranger, when you have such a lover as honest, warm-hearted Jack Garner, who fairly worships the ground you walk on. Every one knows that—and—and pities him."

Dorothy's red lips curled scornfully, and she turned away on her heel.

"He is only a gilder in the bindery," she declared, "while the one I came home with is a grand high-toned, wealthy young fellow, and so aristocratic. He thought nothing of bringing me home in a cab, while Jack Garner would have fainted at the idea. He is so frightened if he spends a dollar of his hard-earned wages. It's no fun going around with a *poor* fellow. I hate them! So there!"

With that Jessie took the bill from her pocket, and told all that poor Jack had said about treating to the ice-cream.

Dorothy looked astounded, but turned the matter off by saying:

"It is a good thing to have him stand treat once in his life-time, I declare!"

But, nevertheless, she felt ashamed deep down in her own heart for the way she had spoken of poor Jack. Still she would not listen to Jessie's admonition, declaring, too, that she meant to go on an excursion on Labor Day with Harry Langdon, even though it made an enemy of Jack for life. She was tired of Jack, anyhow.

"You will rue it if you go with that stranger. Trouble will come of it as sure as you live." Those were Jessie's last words to Dorothy as they parted an hour later, and they rang in Dorothy's brain for many and many a long day afterward; and these two girls, who had been such steadfast friends parted from each other in coldness and in anger for the first time in their lives.

The sun rose bright and golden on the eventful morning, and Dorothy was in high glee as she looked out from her curtained window, and the visions of a joyous day flitted before her.

At two o'clock Langdon put in a prompt appearance, and Dorothy was quite ready, and he could not help but own to himself that she looked as fair and pretty and quite as stylish as any young girl you would meet in a day's travel in her neat navy-blue merino dress, with its white duck vest and broad, white cuffs and sailor collar, and the white sailor hat, with the white silk band about it to match. And nothing could have been more dainty than her neat kid boots and gloves.

Langdon raised his hat to this fair young vision of loveliness with all the gallantry he was capable of, and away they went in high spirits and high glee, and with never a thought in Dorothy's heart of poor Jack toiling at that moment in the book-bindery.

It was a delightful sail down the bay, and when they arrived at their destination they found the island thronged with a merry group of pleasure seekers.

The hours flew by on golden wings. Dusk gathered. Night soon drew her sable curtains, and pinned them with a star.

They dined sumptuously at the Hotel Castleton, and then went back to the picnic grounds, which were ablaze with light and color, resounding to the merry strains of music, the babble of gay voices and joyous laughter, and the sound of feet keeping step in the dance.

Never had Dorothy enjoyed herself so well. Harry Langdon was the prince of escorts. He knew how to make himself agreeable and entertaining. He whispered tender words into his companion's ears, held her little hand, and conveyed to her in a thousand different ways that this was the happiest day of his life, because she was by his side.

At length the hour drew near for the picknickers to leave the grounds, for the boat had already steamed into the dock. In twenty minutes' time she was to start back to the city.

"Have you had a pleasant time, Dorothy?" asked her companion, smiling down into her pleased, flushed face.

"I have had the most pleasant hours of my life!" declared Dorothy. "It has been like heaven here; I am sorry to go. And oh! how dark and drear to-morrow will be in the bindery, after such a pleasant outing here."

"You need not return to the bindery to-morrow unless you wish," whispered Langdon, still holding the girl's little hand in his.

Dorothy's heart beat high. Was handsome Harry Langdon about to propose to her? she wondered.

But no! the words she was waiting for did not fall from his lips, although he had plenty of opportunity as they walked down the gayly festooned path that led to the wharf.

"Perhaps he means to wait until he gets on the boat," she thought, with a fluttering heart.

Poor little Dorothy! there was no one to warn her against him. How was she to realize that the thought of marriage had never entered his head, and that he was of the kind who smile on and flatter women and then ride away, little caring how many broken hearts are left behind?

Dorothy's pretty, innocent face had captivated his fancy, but he would never have dreamed of making her his wife.

As they neared the boat, so great was the crowd clambering on board that Dorothy would have been separated from her companion had she not clung to his arm.

"You need never go back to the book-bindery, Dorothy," he managed to whisper again.

At that moment they stepped aboard the steamer and started toward the upper deck.

It had been a happy day for Dorothy, but a most miserable one for poor Jack. Contrary to his expectations, he finished the task allotted to him much sooner than he had anticipated, and by two o'clock he was ready to quit the book-bindery for the day.

Hurrying home, he quickly changed his clothing, smiling the while as he thought of putting the wish into execution that had been in his heart all day, of joining the crowd up at West Point; and how delighted Dorothy would be to see him—what a surprise it would be to her!

His mother and his cousin watched him out of sight from their humble cottage door, and then turned back to their duties with a sigh. They had hoped that he would spend the day with them.

With a joyful heart Jack boarded the boat for West Point, but when he reached there and found that Dorothy was not among the group, his disappointment knew no bounds.

"My tender-hearted little darling!" he thought. "She would not join them for a day's pleasure because she thought I could not go, and she is having a lonely time of it at home."

Back to the city Jack posted in all haste, and although the hour was late when he reached there—the clocks in the belfries sounding the hour of nine—still he could not refrain from stopping a moment at the cottage, just to let Dorothy know how cruelly fate had tricked him.

To his great consternation, he learned there, from the lady who kept the boarding-house, that Dorothy—his Dorothy—had left the house at two o'clock that afternoon with handsome Mr. Langdon, and that they had started for Staten Island for a day's outing.

He stood quite still, stupefied with amazement too great for words, and a white, awful horror broke over his face and shone in his eyes.

"Tell me about him again!" he cried, hoarsely. "What was he like—this man who took Dorothy away?" And as he listened to the description his face grew stormy with terrible wrath, for it tallied exactly with that of the man who had put Dorothy in the cab and rode away with her.

Like a lightning's flash Jack tore down to the Staten Island wharf, and was just in time to catch the out-going boat. He would surprise them, he told himself, and tear little Dorothy, his promised bride, from his rival's arms, or die in the attempt.

All the way down the bay Jack paced the deck in a tumult of fury that increased with every breath he drew.

The half hour that it took to reach his destination seemed as endless as the pangs of purgatory to lost souls. He never knew how the journey was made, or how he reached the island—flaming with lights on this gala night, and gorgeous with flags and gilded banners.

There were few passengers going down to Staten Island. The steamer had come to take the revellers back to the city, and the gang-plank was no sooner lowered than the crowd rushed aboard with happy laughter and gay repartee. Among the first to gain a foothold on the stairway that led to the upper deck were Harry Langdon and Dorothy; and here, face to face, they met—Jack!

"Unhand that young girl!" he cried, sternly, facing Langdon. "You have no right to be here with her."

Langdon started back, and glanced in haughty amazement at the broad-shouldered, fair-haired young man confronting him.

But without waiting for him to answer, Jack turned to Dorothy, holding out his hands to her, saying huskily:

"Leave him, little one, and come with me."

But Dorothy threw back her head with rising anger.

"How *dare* you, Jack Garner!" she cried, stamping her tiny foot, her blue eyes flashing. "I shall never speak to you again for this—*never*!"

"Step out of our way," cried Dorothy's companion, "and allow this young lady and myself to pass!"

"You shall never pass me with her!" cried Jack, furiously, his hand stealing involuntarily to his breast pocket.

"Step aside; we wish to go on deck!" returned Langdon, haughtily, "and we intend to do so!"

"You will never go on deck with her, unless it be over my dead body!" cried Garner, his face white as death, his voice trembling with excitement, and his brown eyes flashing like living coals of fire.

"*You* can not prevent me," retorted Langdon, in a sneering, contemptuous voice. Then, turning to Dorothy, he added: "I am glad that I am here to stand between you and this intrusive fellow. Come; I will thrust him aside, and we will go on deck, my dear."

The familiarity with which he addressed his companion stung Jack to madness.

"You can pass on deck alone, but not one step shall you proceed with that young girl! Try it at your peril!" shouted Jack, hoarsely.

Langdon did not heed the terrible warning, but attempted to push past with his companion; and in that instant the passengers crowding up from below heard the wild, piercing, terrified cry of the young girl ring out on the night air, and mingled with it the report of a revolver—three shots in quick succession—and the voice of a man crying out in mortal agony: "My God! I am shot!" and the next instant a beautiful, fair-haired girl plunged from the deck down, down into the dark, mad waves, and the seething waters closed quickly over her golden head and white, lovely, childish face.

In an instant there was the most intense excitement and confusion on board the steamer. Young girls fainted, women cried aloud, and strong men stood fairly paralyzed with horror. Great God! the steamer was backing slowly over the spot where the girl had gone down, and where she would reappear. Nothing could save her now.

Chapter IV.

All in an instant the cry rang from lip to lip: "There's a man overboard!" Will he save her? Oh, heavens, is he too late to save the life of the beautiful, rash girl who had plunged into the mad waters scarcely a moment before, or will it mean death for both of them?

He had disappeared beneath the steamer. The next moment that passed seemed the length of eternity to the horrified spectators who lined the dock and the decks, straining their eyes looking down into the dark waters lighted up so fitfully by the pallid moonlight.

He rose, and a great cry broke from every lip. He was alone, and almost instantly he disappeared again. And again he rose, still alone. Every heart sank. People held their breath. Useless, useless to hope. The poor girl's fate was sealed.

Then a mighty cheer broke forth. The waters parted, and they saw him again. This time he was making for the shore, holding in one arm the body of the luckless young girl whom he had risked his own life to save.

Suddenly they heard him utter a sharp cry.

"A rope! A rope! I am sinking!"

In less time than it takes to tell it, a score or more of strong arms hurled one out to him, and he caught it in the nick of time.

Then amidst the greatest excitement he was drawn to the deck with his inanimate burden.

So intense had been the excitement that the passengers who had stood nearest the principals in the bitter quarrel which had taken place had lost track entirely of the fact that a tragedy had almost been enacted in their midst.

And when they began to inquire into the matter no one could tell what had become of the man who had cried out that he had been shot, and they considered it a false alarm.

Had this lovely young girl anything to do with this matter, or was it a coincidence that at the self-same moment she had flung herself into the water?

Meanwhile, kindly hands took the burden from the young man's arms. As he was drawn on deck some one in the crowd cried out in consternation:

"Great Heavens! It's Jack Garner! And the girl whom he has saved is little Dorothy Glenn!"

There was much speculation as to why the girl had attempted to commit suicide; but Jack's friend, a fellow-workman in the book-bindery, declared quickly that it never could have been a case of attempted suicide—the girl must have fallen overboard, and Jack had of course sprung to the rescue.

This looked plausible enough; and what they had all expected to be a great sensation seemed to turn out but an accident pure and simple.

As for Langdon, he had suddenly disappeared in the crowd after striking at the revolver which Jack had drawn upon him and crying out mockingly that he was shot when it was discharged, simply to get Jack into trouble and to get sympathy for himself.

They found it no easy matter to restore the girl to consciousness, and at this juncture an old gentleman, a retired doctor who had been in the cabin when the accident had happened, came hurriedly to her assistance when he heard that she was beyond the skill of those attending her in the ladies' cabin.

"Stand back!" he cried, forcing his way through the crowd of women. "How do you suppose you can bring her to while you stand round her and exclude the air? And by all that's wonderful, although you poured brandy down her throat, no one seemed to know enough to open her dress!"

And forthwith he began hurriedly to open the dress at the throat. But as he did so a low cry broke from his lips, and his florid old face turned deathly white.

"My God, it is she!" he cried, hoarsely; and despite the curious throng about him, the old doctor burst into tears and wept like a child.

He felt that some explanation was due, and in a broken, husky voice he said, pointing to a small, irregular mark over the girl's chest:

"I have been searching for her for sixteen years by night and by day, and finally abandoned all hope of finding her. She—she is not a relative, as you may suppose. A few words will explain:

"Some sixteen years ago I had a beautiful ward, as fair a young girl as ever the sun shone on, and I, a lonely old man who had outlived all his kinsfolk, loved her with all the devotion of my heart.

"She was happy enough in my home—aye, as happy as the day was long, but, like many another young girl, the bitter trial of life came with her first dream of love. She fell in love with a scoundrel. I knew the man better than she, and refused my consent. But young girls are willful, and the upshot of the whole matter was—she eloped with him. It was the most terrible blow of my life. Two years went by, in which I neither saw nor heard of her. Then unexpectedly I received a short, hastily written letter from my heart-broken Alice.

"'When you read this I shall be no more,' she wrote. 'Oh, Doctor Bryan, I have paid the penalty of my folly with my life. I am slowly dying of starvation. For myself, I bow to the fate I have brought upon my own head. But the result of my folly does not rest here. It falls upon the head of an innocent little babe whom I must leave behind me. Oh, Doctor Bryan, this is the prayer that in the last moments of my life I make to you:

"'Plead with the little one's father to let her come to you. If he keeps her, may God in heaven pity her future. He will blast her life as he did mine, or—if it suits his pleasure, he will abandon her on the streets to starve, as I am doing now. If I could think that she would be with you, I would die without this heavy load on my heart. She is so fair and beautiful—my poor little baby! She has only one blemish—the same scar is upon her bosom that is upon mine, and which I have heard you say was upon the bosom of my mother—the birthmark of the three spears.

"'I can not write any more. My hand trembles so that I can scarcely hold the pen.

"'Good-bye, Doctor Bryan. Never forget your poor, heart-broken

ALICE.'

"I searched for her night and day," repeated the old man, with a sob in his voice. "Alice died at sea, and the fate of the little one could not be learned, nor that of the father. I never ceased searching until the last year. Then I said to myself, 'It is useless—useless. Alice's baby is dead.' But I have found her most miraculously at last, thank God!"

This revelation created the most intense excitement among the women, who had listened breathlessly to the *dénouement*.

He had scarcely ceased speaking ere Dorothy opened her eyes. She found to her great consternation a crowd surrounding her.

But in an instant memory returned to her, and with a startled cry she struggled up to a sitting posture, gazing in blank bewilderment upon the crowd that had gathered about her.

"I—I fainted and fell backward," she began; but the old gentleman bent quickly over her, interrupting, hastily:

"Yes, you fell backward and down into the water, my child, and came near drowning. Where is the young man who saved her?" he cried. "Will some one fetch him here at once to me, so that I may thank him? Oh, child, child!" he cried, again bending over Dorothy, "I would have recognized you among ten thousand! You look at me with your mother's eyes!"

"My mother?" cried Dorothy, in awe, thinking that she had not heard aright, or that the gentleman had mistaken her for some one else. "I—I am an orphan; my name is Dorothy Glenn."

The old gentleman did not utter the words that sprang to his lips when she mentioned the name Glenn, though his face darkened for an instant with bitter memory.

"But will you tell me," cried Dorothy, with a piteous sob, "what has become of my escort, Mr. Langdon?"

Nobody seemed to know, and it soon became apparent to everyone—even to the girl herself—that in her peril he had miserably deserted her rather than risk his life to save hers.

"Another young man periled his life for you," some one answered; but who it was Dorothy could not learn, and in that moment she was glad enough to call for Jack—poor, faithful Jack Garner.

But he did not come this time at her bidding. No one told her that he was suffering from a severe contusion on the side of the head, and was scarcely conscious of the message that was sent him at that time.

"You have no need of their protection. From this time henceforth you shall be under my watchful care, little Dorothy;" and very briefly, and to her intense amazement, Mr. Bryan told her the story that he had already related to those about her. "I shall take you home with me," he said, "and you shall never again know want."

To the girl it seemed as though what she had heard was but the wild vagaries of a dream, from which she should awaken presently and find herself back in the old book-bindery with the other girls. But the exclamations of the people who pressed around her congratulating her upon her good fortune, which read so much like a romance, were real enough, for they all knew Doctor Bryan, the wealthy old retired physician, whose elegant country place was just outside of New York.

The loss of Dorothy's handsome lover, who had forsaken her in so shameful a manner, would have been a terrible blow to her had she had time to think and brood over the matter. But this new excitement that had come so suddenly upon her, making part and parcel of her life, threw her thoughts in quite a different channel. How surprised Harry Langdon would be when he heard the wonderful news, and how all the book-bindery girls would hold their breath in astonishment too great for words when she did not come to work on the following day, but got a letter from her instead, explaining the wonderful change in her fortunes! Nadine Holt would be green with envy, and so would the rest of the girls, down in the secret depths of their hearts. There was only one among them who would rejoice because her working-days among them were over, and that was Jessie Staples, who had always declared Dorothy was born to be a real lady.

Chapter V.

Great was the consternation at Gray Gables, as the Bryan mansion was called, when the doctor drove up to the door in the old family carriage, and the housekeeper, looking from the window, saw a young girl seated by his side.

For many years past he had had the strongest aversion to young girls, and it was over sixteen years since one had crossed that threshold. No wonder that the housekeeper was amazed to see him assist her from the carriage and lead her by the hand up the broad walk toward the porch.

"Great Heaven!" cried Mrs. Kemp, as they drew nearer, "it looks like Miss Alice; but it couldn't be her; for long years have passed since—since the night she ran away. It must be her daughter—yes, that is it!"

All of a tremble, she hastened to the door, and flung it open wide. She could see by Mr. Bryan's face that something unusual had occurred, even before her eyes rested on the fair young creature beside him.

"Mrs. Kemp," he said, huskily, "I have here with me one who will surprise you greatly when you hear her name—nay, astound you."

"I can see for myself that she bears a striking resemblance to—to—" and the rest of the sentence was lost in a choking sob.

"I am sorry that I make you feel so bad," said the fresh young voice; and the next instant a pair of plump arms were about the old lady's neck and a soft, velvety cheek was pressed close to hers. "Doctor Bryan has told me all my history," the girl cried in the same breath—"how he has been searching for me all these years, finding me at last; and that I am hereafter to live in this grand old place. And I have been fairly crying with joy all the way up from New York to-day. I could not help but scream with delight, though I know it quite horrified Doctor Bryan, when I saw the house and the magnificent grounds around it. As soon as I take off my hat I want to run into the garden and see the rose-bushes with real roses growing on them, and see what a house is like. I've always lived in a tenement flat or boarding-house."

It made Mrs. Kemp laugh, even through her tears, at the girl's wild enthusiasm. She was like an untrained, untutored child, despite her years, she thought.

The doctor's eyes grew moist as he listened, and during the few days that followed he watched her from his study window with unfeigned delight.

She appeared to him more like a child of seven than a young lady of seventeen.

She was too busy in looking over the place, for the next fortnight, to carry out her intention of writing to the girls.

She seemed to have been lifted into a different world, where the dark past lay far behind her.

At this juncture an event happened which cast a dark shadow over all poor Dorothy's after life.

She was out in the garden one day with Mrs. Kemp, when the doctor joined them, holding a telegram in his hand.

"I have just received word from Harry that he will be here to-morrow," he said, with a pleased expression on his face. "I hope that you will see that a room is put in readiness for him."

"To be sure, sir," responded the housekeeper, with a little courtesy.

His footsteps had scarcely died away ere Dorothy turned eagerly to her companion.

"Who is Harry?" she asked, with all a young girl's curiosity.

"He is a young gentleman who has been studying medicine with Dr. Bryan for the last year," returned the housekeeper, adding, with a slight frown on her comely face: "The doctor is quite fond of him. He has been away for the last three months, and the house has been so nice and quiet without him."

"By the way you speak one wouldn't fancy that you liked this Mr. Harry," laughed Dorothy.

The housekeeper turned grimly away.

"But what is he like?" persisted Dorothy, pursuing the subject.

"Is he young—is he handsome?"

"Handsome is as handsome does," replied Mrs. Kemp, ominously.

"Doesn't he do handsome?" retorted Dorothy, throwing back her curly head with a rich mellow laugh, adding: "But what is he like, anyhow? Is he dark or fair, young or old?"

"No doubt he will strike you as being quite handsome," returned Mrs. Kemp, thoughtfully. "He has very dark eyes and dark waving hair. Young girls would consider him quite good looking."

"And will he, too, live in the house with us?" asked Dorothy, curiously.

"You had better ask Doctor Bryan," responded Mrs. Kemp, evasively.

The next morning, as Dorothy stepped out into the garden to gather flowers for the breakfast-table, she came suddenly upon a young man pacing up and down under the trees with his hands in his pockets, smoking a cigar.

When he heard the light, pattering footsteps he wheeled round, and was just about to raise his hat to the vision of girlish loveliness before him when a low cry of intense astonishment broke from his lips.

"Dorothy Glenn, by all that is wonderful!" he exclaimed.

The amazement was mutual.

"Harry Langdon!" the girl shrieked, turning pale as death.

"What in the name of Heaven brings you to this house?" he cried, hoarsely, catching her wrist and holding it in a tight grip.

"You have no right to know, after the way you deserted me in my peril," flashed Dorothy.

"But how came you here," he repeated, "of all places in the world? I must know!"

The girl briefly outlined how it happened, her anger rising against her questioner with every word; and as he listened his face was a study.

"Dorothy," he said, in his low, smooth voice, "you accuse me of not trying to save you when you fell overboard. But let me speak just one word in my own defense: You remember just what was taking place as we reached the deck. You heard the shot, but you fainted and did not know what happened. The bullet whizzed by me, and I fell back on the deck stunned—unconscious. I did not recover until long after the steamer reached New York. All the people had dispersed long before I returned to consciousness. I made diligent search for you, and to my great horror it soon dawned upon me that not one whom you knew could tell me whither you had gone."

Dorothy was young and guileless, or he could never have fooled her so easily. But the story seemed very plausible to her ears, and her face brightened.

It was a great load lifted from her heart—her trustful belief that handsome Mr. Langdon had not been false to her after all.

"Now, Dorothy, I have something to say to you," he began. "Walk down this path with me, for you must listen intently to what I have to say to you. I have a little confession to make to you, and a favor to ask, and surely you are too kind of heart and too good a friend to me to refuse. I had intended telling you this upon our return on the boat. My name is not Harry Langdon, as you have believed, but Harry Langdon Kendal.

"I am studying medicine with Doctor Bryan, instead of law, as I once led you to believe. And as to the great expectations I told you about, I confess that they exist only in my mad hopes that Doctor Bryan, who is alone in the world, without kith or kin, might take a fancy to leave me something some day. He does not know of my rash wager, and that by losing it I was forced to go to New York and place myself on a street car as conductor for a while. He would disapprove of it if he knew, and, Dorothy, you must never tell him—promise me that here and now—he must never know that we have ever met before!"

Dorothy did not hesitate to give him the required assurance, for which he thanked her so profusely that it brought the warm blushes in a flood-tide to the girl's dimpled cheeks; and Mrs. Kemp wondered why Dorothy looked so happy as she entered the house.

Left to himself, Kendal paced excitedly under the trees, puffing away vigorously at his cigar.

"A devil of a fix this," he muttered, setting his white teeth hard together. "Great Heaven! this is a romance in real life more strangely weird than any fiction. Who would have thought of finding this girl here, of all persons in the world, and under such circumstances! And then, to make matters worse, I have been making violent love to the girl. It was all very well to make desperate love to the little New York working-girl, but to make love to Miss Glenn, the doctor's *protégée*, is quite another matter. I shall be expected to ask for her hand in marriage, of course, and she without a dollar. No, thanks! I'd rather that some other fellow would woo and win the little blue-eyed fairy. When it comes to marrying I must have a girl with money, who can put up the needful for both if necessary. If she will only keep my secret I will be but too grateful!"

Meanwhile, Dorothy had stolen up to her own room, and at that moment was standing before the mantel, resting her elbows on it, her dimpled chin upon her hands, gazing wistfully into the mirror's depths at the lovely young face it reflected.

"Oh, how my cheeks burn!" she cried, excitedly, "and how my heart thumps even yet. I was sure he would hear it. I thought I should never see him again, but it is fate that brings us together here. I shall always believe in it firmly and truly after this. He cares for me. He as much as told me so on the night that we went to the moonlight picnic on Staten Island, and the fortune-teller who told my fortune said—when all of us bindery girls visited her one day—'I see a short journey for you, miss—a dark young man and a marriage-ring;'" and for the next ten minutes Dorothy capered around the room, dancing in such hoidenish, girlish glee that she would fairly have shocked the old housekeeper could she have seen her. "It's all coming true!" cried Dorothy, breathlessly, to herself. But not one thought did she give to poor Jack, whose betrothal-ring she carried pinned to her pocket.

Chapter VI.

How the hours passed up to luncheon time Dorothy never afterward realized, her foolish little heart was in such a flutter of excitement.

She knew she should meet Harry at the table, and oh! it would be so hard to pretend before Doctor Bryan and the stern, keen-eyed old housekeeper that they were strangers.

She had but two dresses as yet, which the housekeeper had provided her with, and she tried on each of them in succession to see which looked best on her.

Which should it be? The pale-blue merino or the rose-pink cashmere?

After much studying and slipping on and off, Dorothy decided upon wearing the rose-pink.

She was scarcely dressed ere the luncheon bell rang.

Taking up her handkerchief, Dorothy flew down the stairway, pausing before the doorway to catch her breath and to summon courage to enter.

But the longer she stood there the more difficult it seemed to get courage enough to open the door and face the music. At length she heard Doctor Bryan inquire surprisedly of Mrs. Kent:

"Where can Dorothy be, I wonder?"

And the next instant they heard a faint voice exclaim:

"Here I am, please."

And, turning to see from whence the sound proceeded, they all saw distinctly that the door was open the space of an inch, and that a human eye was applied to the crack, while four little fingers clutched it frantically to keep it open.

"Come in, Dorothy," commanded Mr. Bryan, inwardly highly amused at the girl's bashfulness in venturing in when she saw a stranger seated at the board.

Dorothy opened the door, stumbled over the mat, and, with a face red as a beet, walked awkwardly to the table and took her seat, which happened to be directly opposite Harry's.

She did not dare for the life of her to look at him, for she knew that his black eyes were bent upon her. She felt them scorching down into her soul.

"Dorothy," said Mr. Bryan, pompously, "allow me to present to you my young friend, Mr. Kendal."

"I am right glad to see him, sir," said Dorothy, faintly, without raising her eyes.

Noticing her embarrassment, Doctor Bryan quickly turned the conversation into another channel; but he soon observed that his young friend was looking at the girl across the table, almost convulsed with laughter.

It took but one glance that way to see the cause.

In her great confusion Dorothy was making dire efforts to eat her soup with a fork, catching occasionally a stray bean.

"Remove the soup plates!" roared the doctor to the servant who stood in waiting, and who was also grinning at the girl's discomfiture.

It was the most confusing meal that Dorothy had ever sat down to.

And when she arose from the table she was far hungrier than when she sat down.

She had scarcely eaten a good solid mouthful.

Oh, it was so hard to act out such a falsehood as handsome Harry had prevailed upon her to do.

During the fortnight that followed, she became more used to the situation, but it was no little wonder, both to the housekeeper and Doctor Bryan, what excellent friends they were getting to be in so short a time.

It could not be that they were falling in love with each other; and the doctor looked rather serious at the last thought.

As for Dorothy, it was quite a clear case; she was deeply in love with Harry Kendal. Like all girls, her day-dreams were rosy. It was so sweet to wander with him through the grand grounds surrounding Gray Gables, or sit in the sunshine in the clover meadow beyond, with the babbling brook at their feet, and the great branches of the oak trees over their heads, and listen to him while he read such sweet poems to her—poems of how some lover loved a lassie, and how bright was their future.

But still there was a change in him; he wasn't just like he used to be when she was only Dorothy Glenn, working for her living in the book-bindery. And just to show him that she did not notice the change, and did not care, she was so gay and hoidenish, so full of repartee and laughter, that she saw him open his eyes in wonder more than once; and Doctor Bryan gave her the *soubriquet* of "Madcap Dorothy," which seemed to suit her exactly.

There was no prank that could ever have entered a roguish girl's brain which she did not play upon Kendal.

This phase of her character rather annoyed Kendal than pleased him; and it seemed to him that she took a special delight in teasing him. She hid his slippers, slipped briars into his couch, turned tack-points upward in his lounging chairs, and substituted periodicals a month old for his morning journals and magazines, until he almost grew to detest her for becoming the torment of his life. Shrewd as he was in the ways of young girls, he did not know that this is the course which many a young girl pursues toward a young man with whom she has fallen in love, and would not have him know it for the whole world.

If there was anything which Kendal detested, it was a girl who was always on the lookout to turn every word and action into a joke. He preferred them modest and flower-like; still, he was in duty bound to treat her as well as he could because she was under that roof.

And there was another reason why he began to abhor Dorothy. Before her appearance on the scene, there had been a wild hope in his heart that some day he might possibly inherit a good portion of Doctor Bryan's money. For two years or more he had left no stone unturned to get into the old gentleman's good graces.

True, Dorothy was as much of a stranger to Doctor Bryan as he himself was, but who knew but that, by some freak of unlucky fate, he might take a notion to leave the girl all of his fortune? He wished to Heaven she had never crossed the threshold of Gray Gables.

At this turn of affairs it occurred to him that it would not be a bad idea to test the old gentleman's friendship for himself; and the greatest of all tests, he believed, was to borrow money from him. If Doctor Bryan refused this little favor, he reasoned to himself, all his hopes in regard to inheriting the old gentleman's money, in time to come, would be dashed. He would ask him for a small loan; and on the very day this occurred to him he proceeded to put it into execution, saying to himself:

"'He either fears his fate too much,Or his deserts are small,Who fears to put it to, the touchTo win or lose it all.'"

He knew that he should find the doctor in his study directly after luncheon, and here he presented himself with some trepidation.

"Come in," called the doctor, in answer to his knock.

"Oh, it's *you*, is it, Harry?" he exclaimed, placing a chair for him, which the young man took rather awkwardly.

"It is not often I trouble you in your study, sir," began Harry, "but I have something of importance to say to you, and I beg that you will pardon the intrusion. I chose a time when we will be least apt to be interrupted."

"I wouldn't advise you to begin it if it will take long to tell," said Mr. Bryan, "for we might be interrupted at any moment. I am expecting an old friend, who is to accompany me on a horse-back ride. He ought to have been here by this time."

Harry fidgeted nervously about in his chair. It required something of an effort to make his request carelessly.

"You are the only one," he began, a little disconcertedly, "I feel sure, who can help me in my present dilemma."

The old doctor wheeled suddenly around in his chair, and all in an instant the object of the young man's visit flashed over his mind.

"To my mind he is come to tell me that he has fallen head over heels in love with little Dorothy, and wants to marry her;" and with the thought a broad smile crept up to the lips the white beard covered.

He had never been in love himself—but, for all that, he always sympathized with young folks in their tender affairs of the heart, and many a secret sigh escaped his lips for the lost opportunities of the past.

"Well," he began, brusquely, "why don't you proceed, my boy?"

"It is such a delicate matter," began Kendal, "that I scarcely know how to frame the words. You have always been so kind to me in the past, that the remembrance of it has led me to dare hope that your goodness will not desert me in the present emergency."

"Well," said the old gentleman, rather enjoying the young man's evident discomfiture, "pray go on."

"The boon I have to ask," began Kendal, "will either make or mar my future."

"Is it so bad as that?" returned the old gentleman with assumed innocence.

"You could never imagine what it is that I wish to ask," continued the young man.

"I might guess, perhaps," laughed the doctor, with a roguish twinkle in his eye.

"Surely you—you couldn't have noticed the one great wish of my heart," gasped Kendal. "I—"

At that moment the expected visitor was announced.

"Come and see me in my library this evening," said Doctor Bryan, grasping the young man's hand, "and we will talk over the matter you have so much at heart, and I will give you my answer in regard to it."

"You are too good, sir," cried Kendal, in bewilderment.

At that moment the entrance of the visitor put a stop to all further conversation, and Kendal arose and took his leave after an exchange of greetings.

"How could he possibly have divined that I was thinking of asking him for money?" he pondered.

He heard Dorothy singing at the top of her voice in the drawing-room, and he turned on his heel in the hallway, and walked in an opposite direction with a frown of impatience on his face.

Dorothy saw him pass the door, and she bit her lip with vexation.

"Of course he heard me playing on the piano, for I thumped as loud as ever I could; but he did not come in. It seems to me he is trying 'to cool off,' as we girls in the bindery used to say."

Dorothy tiptoed over to the window as she heard the front door slam after him, and if he had looked back he would have seen a very defiant though tear-stained face peering earnestly after him from behind the lace curtains.

Kendal walked disconsolately enough through the spacious grounds and out into the main road, little dreaming that a strange fate was drawing him onward with each step he took.

He had traveled a mile or more over the country road, when suddenly he was startled by the sound of horses' hoofs.

The next instant, from around the bend in the road, a horse dashed riderless, covered with foam, and so near him that he had to spring aside or its hoofs would have been buried in his brain. One glance, and a cry of horror broke from his lips. It was Doctor Bryan's horse.

Great God! where was he? Kendal realized that there had been a terrible accident, and that at that moment the doctor lay dying—perhaps dead—by the road-side.

In all haste he rushed down the road in the direction whence the horse had come, and around the first bend he beheld the prostrate figure of Doctor Bryan lying covered with dust, his friend bending over him.

In an instant he was by his side. One glance, and his worst fears were realized—the old gentleman had been mortally injured—he was dying. He held out his hand when he saw Kendal bending over him, and nodded assent as his companion briefly and hurriedly related how the terrible accident had come about.

"I was just about to go for you," said the friend. "The doctor has something to say to you. Surely it was the work of Providence that you happened along just now."

Kendal bent over the prostrate form.

"I—I am dying, Harry!" gasped the doctor; "but that—of which we were—talking—this—afternoon—is—uppermost—in—my—mind. You—you—wished—me—to—give my—consent—to—to—your—wooing—and wedding little—Dorothy. I—give—it—to you—here—and—now—with—my—blessing—for—I—know—she—cares—for you. Six months—from—to-day—at—noon—my—will—must be read; and on that day you—must marry her—if ever—aye—you must—be wedded—ere that noon-hour—shall have waned. Then—then—within that hour—you shall know—the contents of—my will; and—remember, too, that—it—is—irrevocable!"

Harry Kendal reeled back, like one dazed by an awful blow.

The suddenness of this affair had taken his breath away. But before he could raise his voice in protest, or utter one word of the terrible mistake which the old gentleman was laboring under, Doctor Bryan breathed his last, and he found himself betrothed, as it were, to Dorothy, and by the most terrible mistake that ever a man labored under.

Chapter VII.

A fortnight had passed since the fatal accident in Brighton Woods, and life at Gray Gables had once more resumed the even tenor of its regular routine.

The first words that Doctor Bryan had gasped out to his friend, when he regained consciousness and found himself fatally injured, were:

"Tell—tell—them at home—that—everything—must go—on—the same—until—after—my will—has—been read—and that—must not be—until—six—months—after—my—decease."

The sudden loss of Doctor Bryan, the kind-hearted old gentleman who had raised her from poverty to great wealth, was a severe blow to Dorothy. For in that short length of time she had learned to love him, as a daughter might have done, with all the strength of her passionate, girlish heart.

The old housekeeper and the servants, who had been in his employ a quarter of a century or more, mourned for him and refused to be comforted.

Great was the excitement in the household when the friend who had accompanied Doctor Bryan on that fatal ride broke to them the strange compact between the doctor and Kendal, to which he had been a witness.

He readily decided that it was best not to tell Dorothy the exact situation of affairs, and that it would probably be more in accordance with a young girl's romantic idea of marriage for Kendal to woo her on his own account, and gain her consent, ere he breathed to her that this was Doctor Bryan's wish.

And this was the course that Kendal followed. He allowed fully a month to transpire ere he made the slightest advances to her. Long and carefully he had thought the matter over in his own mind, and had concluded that there was no way out of the strange betrothal into which he had been forced, as it were, against his will.

He made up his mind to accept the situation gracefully and become engaged to Dorothy, and if he found out that she had not been remembered in the old gentleman's will, he could break it without one word of warning or the least compunction. He noticed, too, that Dorothy was growing quite shy of him of late. She had been quite fond of him in the past; it would never do to allow her to grow indifferent to him. He made up his mind to settle the matter—as far as the engagement was concerned—at the first opportunity; and one presented itself on the very day he made this resolve.

Dorothy was in the conservatory that afternoon, when he suddenly surprised her, stealing up on tip-toe behind her, clasped her in his arms, holding his hands over her eyes, whispering:

"Guess who it is, Dorothy."

The struggle to escape those firm arms suddenly ceased. The girl was dumbfounded with amazement.

"Is it—can it be you, Harry—Mr. Kendal?" she gasped, breathlessly.

"Do you wish it were some one else, Dorothy?" he whispered, releasing her from his arms, but catching her hands in a tight clasp and looking eagerly down into her eyes.

The girl's face flushed burning red, and her gaze fell beneath a pair of dark eyes that seemed to search into her very soul. But in an instant she recovered something of her old hoidenish composure; and in that moment she remembered, too, how he had seemed to slight her of late, and her pride rebelled hotly.

"How dare you frighten me so, Harry Kendal?" she cried, drawing back and stamping her little foot, her blue eyes blazing angrily.

"Are you so very displeased?" he inquired, reproachfully, adding quietly: "If that is the case, I beg your pardon. I shall never so trespass again;" and he dropped her hand and turned away, walking moodily to the window.

"Gracious! I have done it now!" thought Dorothy, repenting on the instant; and, as he made no effort to turn around or speak to her again, she advanced slowly to where he stood idly drumming upon the window-sill.

"I wasn't so very angry," she began, hesitatingly, picking nervously at the blue ribbons which tied her long, curling hair. "I said I wasn't so very angry!" repeated Dorothy, nervously. He heard her, but never turned his head, and Dorothy was at a loss what to say next to mend matters. "Would you like a rose?" she stammered.

"Thanks—no!" replied Kendal, shortly, still without turning his head. Then, after a brief pause:

"Or would you like me to show you a new book of poems I just bought?"

"You needn't mind. Pray don't trouble yourself," he responded.

Dorothy looked at him an instant, quite as though she was ready to cry; then the best thing that could have happened, under the circumstances, came to her relief.

She grew angry.

"I wouldn't show you the book now, to save your life!" she cried, her breath coming and going in panting gasps, and her cheeks flaming as scarlet as the deep-red rose she had brought him as a peace-offering; "nor would I give you this flower. I'd tear it up and stamp it beneath my feet first—you are so mean!"

He turned with a very tantalizing smile, and looked at her out of the corners of his eyes.

She had hidden her face in her hands, but by the panting of her breast he saw that she was weeping, that a storm of sobs was shaking her childish frame.

He stooped and passed his arm lightly around the slim waist, his hand holding hers.

Dorothy trembled.

"Won't you let me comfort you?" he asked, in that low, winning voice of his.

The thought flashed across Dorothy's brain that, if she pushed him from her, he would never again put his arms about her, and she meekly endured the caress for an instant; and not being repulsed, he grew bold enough to kiss the rosy cheek that peeped out from between the white fingers.

"I have something to say to you, Dorothy," he whispered. "It is this: I love you! Will you be my wife?"

Dorothy had always imagined just how a lover should propose, but she had never imagined anything so commonplace as this.

He stooped to caress her again, but she drew back.

"You frighten me!" she cried; and at these words he instantly released her.

"It is alarming—being kissed—and especially when you're not used to it. But that does not answer my question. Will you marry me, or will you not?"

"I don't know!" cried Dorothy, faintly. "You mustn't ask me; you must talk to Mrs. Kemp about it."

"I might talk to Mrs. Kemp about changing my room in the house, or ask her concerning anything belonging to the household, but I couldn't think of asking her to find me a wife and to seal the bargain for me. The 'Yes' or

'No' must be said by the girl herself, as she is the one who is to live with me and to make the best or the worst of the bargain through life. Now, Dorothy, I want a plain, straightforward answer. Tell me, will you be my bride?"

She colored and smiled, and the sort of shy half fear which always assailed her at his approach came over her now more strongly than ever, and the quick blood came rushing to her finger-ends.

"I—don't know what to say!" gasped Dorothy. "I couldn't marry anybody, I think."

His arms dropped from about her.

"Am I to understand, then," he asked, in a constrained voice, "that you refuse me?"

"Oh, I don't know!" cried Dorothy, melting into fresh, quick tears. "I—I—should want to ask somebody about it first before I said 'Yes.'"

He had quite believed that she would accept him on the spot the moment he proposed, and her failure to do this made him almost catch his breath in astonishment.

This uncertainty in the matter gave more zest to his ardor.

"You dislike me?" he questioned, wondering if that could possibly be.

"Oh, no, no! I like you. Won't you believe me?"

He stepped back and looked at her with a sarcastic smile—looked at the little figure leaning against the fountain, with one hand resting on the rim of it, the other held out imploringly toward him.

"Believe you? Why do you insist upon making me uncivil?" he replied. "I do *not* believe you! I dare say you fancy that you are telling the truth; but if another man were to come on the scene with a few thousands a year more, and a higher position in the social scale, you would have a very different answer for him at your tongue's end."

He looks at her—looks at the innocently wooing arms—at the tear-stained, dimpled, tremulous face, and, now that he thinks that he can not win her, all in an instant he falls madly in love with her.

"You must answer me, here and now!" he cried; but Dorothy turned from him, and, like a startled fawn, slipped through his outstretched hands, through the conservatory, and out of the corridor beyond, leaving him staring after her, his handsome face pale with emotion.

Dorothy never paused until she reached her own room.

She closed and locked the door with trembling hands and beating heart; then, after the fashion of young girls, she laughed and cried hysterically all in a breath, dancing around the room in a mad fashion, clapping her hands and sobbing out:

"Oh, at last—at last, my hero, my ideal has turned from a block of marble to human clay, and tells me that he loves me and wants me to be his wife—me—a silly little thing like me!" and she paused before the glass, wondering what he saw in the pink-and-white face reflected there to love forever and ever. She wished she knew.

Chapter VIII.

Dorothy's merriment was soon interrupted by a loud knock at the door, and when she opened it, panting with her exertion of dancing around the room, she found Mrs. Kemp standing there, with a white, frightened face.

"What in the world is the matter here, child?" she cried, in alarm. "I was afraid there were burglars, or Heaven knows what, up here in this room."

Dorothy burst into a peal of laughter that amazed the old lady and made the very walls echo with her bright young voice.

"Oh, something so funny has just happened!" she gasped. "You will be as much surprised as I was, Mrs. Kemp, when you hear it."

The housekeeper knew just what had happened, for, although unknown to Dorothy, she was in the conservatory when she had entered; but before she could make her presence known Kendal had appeared upon the scene, and the proposal of marriage had followed so quickly upon the heels of it that she felt she could not leave without embarrassing both, so she waited there until they had quitted the conservatory.

As soon as she thought it practicable she followed Dorothy to her room to congratulate her, and the sight that met her view surprised her—the girl's face, instead of being flushed with tell-tale blushes and covered with confusion, as she had expected, was convulsed with laughter.

"Oh, do come in!" cried Dorothy, excitedly. "I have something that I want to tell you—I want you to decide for me what is best to do."

"I will give you the best advice I can," said the old housekeeper, drawing the girl down beside her on the sofa, and putting her arm about her.

"I've just had a—a proposal of—of marriage. There! the whole secret is out!" cried Dorothy, breathlessly.

But the good old lady did not look a particle amazed, much to Dorothy's surprise.

"You do not ask me who it is that wants me," cried the girl, in bitter disappointment.

Mrs. Kemp smiled.

"It was very easy to see that for myself," she responded. "Every one could tell that Harry Kendal was very fond of you, my dear, and that sooner or later he would ask you to marry him. But tell me, what answer did you make him?"

"I—I ran away without making any answer at all," confessed Dorothy, shamefacedly. "I thought I could write him a note and put my answer in it—ever so much better than to look up into his face and tell him," she faltered. "I wonder that girls can ever say 'Yes' right up and down, then and there; it seems so bold a thing to do. Why, I never felt so embarrassed in my life. When I tried to say something my tongue cleaved to the roof of my mouth. I trembled from head to foot, and—oh, gracious!—he must have heard how my heart thumped. I know I must have acted like the greatest simpleton the world ever held. Wasn't it wonderful to think that he wanted to marry me? I can't understand it."

"It is not so very wonderful, but very natural," responded Mrs. Kemp, warmly. "I do not know whether it is wise to tell you so or not, but you are really beautiful. Every one thinks so hereabouts. And then you are not too young to marry—you are seventeen."

"But I'm not a bit wise," persisted Dorothy.

"You are quite wise enough to suit the exacting eyes of love," declared the housekeeper, reassuringly, "and that is all that is needed. The greatest of all questions, however, is: Do you think you care for Mr. Kendal? Let me tell you two things, my dear—never marry a man whom you do not love; and if the one whom you do love asks you, do not coquet with him."

"Will you help me to write the note to him?" cried Dorothy, drawing up a hassock, and slipping down upon it at her companion's feet. "I want to write it stiff and proud, as though I didn't care much, and I want to get all the big words in it that I can."

"Of course I will help you," replied Mrs. Kemp. "But it's many a year since I wrote a love letter, and I'm a little awkward at it now. But as long as it conveys the idea of 'Yes' to him, your ardent lover will think it the grandest epistle that ever a young girl wrote."

Such a time as there was over that letter!

Over and over again it was copied, this word erased, and that word inserted, until at the very best it looked more like the map of Scotland than anything else.

Dorothy was terribly in earnest over it.

One would almost have thought, to have seen her, that her life was at stake over the result of it; but at last it was finished, and one of the servants was called to take it to Mr. Kendal's room.

Harry was pacing restlessly up and down when it was delivered to him. He took it eagerly and broke the seal, for he had recognized Dorothy's cramped, school-girl chirography at once.

"She is mine!" he cried, triumphantly; and with the knowledge that he had won her without a doubt, his ardor suddenly cooled; he did not know whether he was pleased or sorry over the result of his wooing.

After he had read the letter over carefully, he fell to scrutinizing the chirography.

"The first thing I shall have to do will be to teach the girl how to write a legible letter," he thought.

Only the day before she had written a letter to Jack, which contained but the few words that she was well and happy, and that a great change of fortune had come into her life. But the letter bore neither date, postmark, nor signature, and he could not tell where it had been posted.

But it was the first intimation which Jack had had that she was in the land of the living, and to have seen his face as he read it would have touched a heart of stone.

Tears sprang to his eyes, strong young man though he was, and he covered the half-written page with burning kisses. To him those irregular, girlish strokes were dearer than anything else this wide world held, because they were Dorothy's.

Although she had suddenly disappeared, and all her friends had turned against her in the bindery, declaring that she had eloped with the handsome, dark-eyed stranger, he still believed her true. He had been searching for her ever since, without rest—almost without food—day and night, until he had almost worn himself out.

He believed she was in the city somewhere, that she had been ashamed to return to the bindery after that scene on the steamer, and had gone some place else to work, and he walked the streets for hours at a time, searching for her among the crowds of working-girls as they trooped down Broadway in laughing, chattering groups each evening, only to turn away, alas! disappointed and almost broken-hearted.

And thus another month dragged its slow length by. It was well that he did not know where Dorothy was, or what was occurring during those days of suspense.

The news of her betrothal to handsome Harry Kendal had spread over the entire village, and it caused no little sensation in Yonkers, on the outskirts of which Gray Gables was situated; for every one had said that this was the way the affair would terminate when the doctor brought the handsome young stranger beneath the same roof with dashing, dark-eyed Harry Kendal, the *beau-idéal* of all the girls.

But there was some disappointment when they learned that the marriage would not take place for nearly half a year yet.

"It's all very well *now*, with rosy love in their sky; but delays are dangerous," said some people, shaking their heads ominously.

Dorothy was as happy as the day was long, for she was learning to fairly adore her lover, and treated him in a childish fashion which rather amused every one who saw them together.

If he brought her a box of *bonbons* she would spring up and throw her arms about his neck, like an overgrown baby, and end by giving him a hearty smack straight on the lips—no matter who was present.

Once or twice he had attempted to expostulate with her sternly, coldly, but his manner so frightened her that she almost went into hysterics, and turning away with a white, set face, he would say no more.

What could he expect? he asked himself, grimly. He had asked an untutored school-girl to be his wife—he had sown the wind, and now he was commencing to reap the whirlwind. Every one else seemed highly delighted over Dorothy's childish, romping ways; but as for himself, they rankled upon his proud, sensitive, haughty nature.

He loved her in such a cool, lordly manner, and poor little Dorothy was always impressed with his superiority. She was obliged to acknowledge that Harry Kendal was her master. She could never make him her slave.

At this juncture an event happened that changed the current of poor Dorothy's after life. It was election night, and the bonfires were blazing on hill and vale, and all the young people of the village were wild with enthusiasm over the affair.

A great bonfire had been built in the road in front of Gray Gables, as had been the custom for years. The old doctor had been very patriotic.

"This year there is no one to cheer the boys on in their good work," said the housekeeper, sadly, as they were all standing out on the porch.

"I'll do it," cried Dorothy, and before the echo of her words had died away rousing cheers broke from her lips, that were answered back heartily by the crowd assembled with an enthusiastic "Hip, hip, hurrah, and a tiger!" for the young lady of Gray Gables.

Kendal was mortally angry, and his face grew dark. He strode up to her and grasped her shoulder, his fingers unwittingly clinching deeply into the soft flesh.

"For Heaven's sake, stop, you tom-boy!" he cried. "Stop disgracing me!"

She flung up her little head proudly. If he had spoken to her alone she would not have cared, but before all these people! Oh, it was unbearable. She would resent it if it killed her.

Chapter IX.

For an instant their eyes met—his blazing dark and stormy in the clear, bright moonlight, and his face white and wrathy; even his hands were clinched fiercely.

All in an instant the old fire and pride blazed up in Dorothy Glenn's heart.

"You shall not coerce me as if I were your very slave!" she said, smiting her little hands together and pushing him from her, forgetting in her great anger whether or not her action accorded well with her dignity. "They cheered me, and I shall respond!" and before he could utter one word of protest she had sped like a swallow down the graveled path and out through the great arched gateway into the very midst of the throng of merry maidens and young men who were gathered with hilarious glee around the roaring bonfire.

The great stacks of burning barrels and boxes sent forth a glare of red light and columns of flame shooting skyward, lighting up the scene with a grand, weird beauty that lent a splendor to the night.

Great sparks flew heavenward, and the crackling sounds mingled with the rousing cheers that rent the air.

They all saw Dorothy, the village favorite, flying toward them, and the great throng parted to make way for her. Then the sport of the evening went on with renewed vigor.

"Pile on the barrels!" cried one enthusiastic fellow. "Whether the election is going Democratic or Republican, let's all give three cheers for the incoming governor!" and a loud huzza that made the old town ring broke from a couple of hundred throats, but mingled with it sounded a wild cry of mortal terror in Dorothy's agonizing voice.

"Oh, my God! my eyes—my eyes! the sparks—the sparks have flown into them! They are burning! Oh, God!"

And with that agonizing cry she fell backward in a dead faint in the midst of the dazed crowd.

In an instant the greatest confusion prevailed, and the shouts of laughter were turned to sobs of wailing.

Kind hands quickly raised her and bore her to the house. We will pass gently, dear reader, over the two weeks that followed, for Gray Gables was buried in the deepest sorrow.

One of the most pitiful calamities that ever could have befallen a human being had happened to beautiful, hapless Madcap Dorothy. Poor child! she was blind!

Never again would she see the light of the golden sunshine—never again see the green, waving grass and the budding flowerets—never see the blue sky, with its fleecy clouds, or the heavens at night blazing with the soft, pale light of the twinkling stars—never again look upon a human face. But while her life lasted she would grope through a world of darkness—blind!

The shock had been terrible to both Mrs. Kemp and Harry Kendal, and oh! in her pitiful condition how she clung to them!

"You will not throw me off now because I am blind, Harry?" she wailed, laying her head against his bosom and weeping as she had never before wept in all her young life.

"No!" he said, huskily; and that promise reassured her.

She clasped her white arms around his neck and clung to him in the abandonment of her pitiful woe.

She was wild and willful Madcap Dorothy no longer.

During the first days of her trial friends flocked to see her, but as they grew used to the situation they dropped off, and she was left with only the old housekeeper, and her lover, and the servants of Gray Gables for her companions.

At first she grieved over the terrible calamity with all the bitterness of her soul, then by degrees she became reconciled to it.

But the one great anxiety of her life was in regard to her lover. He had promised to love her still and be true to her; but would he—would he? The very thought alarmed her soul and became the one terror of her life.

The blind are always acute in other senses.

She felt intuitively, as the days wore on, that he was growing cold toward her. It was pitiful to see her grasp the hands of the little maid that had been engaged to take care of her, and hear her beg her to dress her prettily, and to see that every curl was in place, and the lace at her throat and sleeves fresh and white.

"Oh, Katy, do I look very horrible?" she would whisper, in a breath of intense agony, over and over again a hundred times during the day. "Are there not cruel scars on my face? Oh, God! the terrible fire burned my eyes to their sockets—dry. Surely I must be a thing so horrible to the sight, that people who see me turn away quickly, suppressing a cry on their lips. Is it not so?"

"Oh, no, miss! Believe me, there is not a scar on your pretty face. Your cheeks have lost a little of their bloom, that is all, and the white lids gently cover your poor eyes, and the long lashes sweep your cheeks. You look as though you were walking in your sleep."

"But tell me, Katy," sobbed Dorothy, "do you think Harry does—do you think Harry could love me as well as before?"

"And why not, miss?" returned the little maid. "Surely, with your affliction, he should love you doubly more than he ever did before. You needn't fear about my not dressing you in your prettiest, Miss Dorothy. Sure, I'm always making little bows and fancy things for your dresses, and twining the loveliest of flowers in your pretty golden hair!"

Dorothy would smile faintly, piteously, and sigh ever so gently.

Oh, God! the pity of groping around those rooms day in and day out! What mattered it if she sat by the open window, as she had been wont to do? She could not see her lover strolling under the maple-trees, even though she heard his voice and knew he was there.

She would look upon his darkly handsome face never again in this world; and at times Dorothy's soul grew so bitter over her terrible misfortune that she wished she could die. As for Harry Kendal, after the first shock of intense pity over Dorothy's unhappy fate was past, he grew morose and taciturn.

It was bad enough to wed a maiden whom he did not love with all his heart and soul—such as he had heard it expressed in the burning, eloquent words of authors and poets—but to go through life with a blind woman at his side! The very thought made his soul shudder and grow sick within him.

He dared not make any attempt to break their engagement just then, for public sentiment was strongly with the girl; but the chains that bound him to her began to grow very heavy.

Surely she ought not wish to hold him in thraldom now. It was irksome for him to go where she was, to passively receive her caresses as well as attempt to stay her burning tears, and to be obliged to assure her over and over again, with every breath, that he would be sure to be true to her.

Alas! what a slender thread of circumstances in this world changes our fate for weal or for woe!

Ever since the accident had happened, and the doctors had all pronounced the terrible decree that poor Dorothy would go through life totally blind, the poor old housekeeper had been maturing a plan in her head which she thought would be a world of comfort to the poor girl.

Mrs. Kemp had a niece whom she had kept at boarding-school all the girl's life, for she was an orphan, and she said to herself: "How grand a plan it would be to bring the girl to Gray Gables to be a companion to Dorothy until she marries!"

Her niece was a bright, gay creature, and would be just the one to cheer Dorothy up.

Mrs. Kemp concluded to put this plan into execution at once, as there was no one to say nay in regard to it, and she wrote to her niece to come on without delay, little dreaming that this one action would prove the curse of three lives—aye, the bitterest curse that ever wrung a human heart, and that heart poor, hapless Dorothy's.

Ah, me! how often in this world that which we mean for the greatest good turns out the source of the cruelest woe.

Dorothy heard of the plan, and agreed to it eagerly.

"Oh, thank you—thank you for the happy thought, Mrs. Kemp!" she cried; "for I am lonely—so pitifully lonely. Yes, I would give the world for a girl of my own age to be a companion to me until—until I marry Harry."

Kendal received the intelligence with a look of interest in his eyes.

"When does your niece come, Mrs. Kemp?" he inquired.

"I expect Iris to come to-morrow," she replied. And on the following afternoon Iris Vincent arrived.

The carriage met her at the depot. Harry went for her himself. Dorothy stood at the window, with Katy, her faithful little maid, awaiting Iris' coming with the greatest impatience.

At last the carriage stopped before the arched gateway, and she heard the sound of voices, then a peal of light, girlish laughter ringing out above all the rest.

"Has she come?" whispered Dorothy.

"Yes, miss," murmured the little maid, in a low voice.

"What is she like?" questioned Dorothy, eagerly.

Faithful little Katy looked out of the window, then at Dorothy, a sudden lump rising in her throat and a great fear at her heart.

She dared not tell her that the strange young girl was as beautiful as a poet's dream—slim as a young willow, dressed in the height of fashion, and, worse still—oh, a thousand times worse!—she was bringing all her charms to bear upon handsome Harry Kendal, who was walking up the graveled walk with her.

"Why don't you answer me?" cried Dorothy, impatiently.

"She—she is about your height," stammered Katy, "and—and she is very plain, and—and not so fair as you;" and Katy lifted up her face to heaven, clasping her hands, whispering to herself: "May God forgive me! It is my first lie!"

CHAPTER X.

Mrs. Kemp hastened to the door to meet her niece, and the next moment the echo of a gay young voice, bright and joyous, rang through the corridor.

"She must be a very happy girl, and light of heart," sighed Dorothy.

Katy, the maid, had nothing to say. Much to Dorothy's surprise, they did not come to the room in which she was awaiting them, and she heard them go on to the drawing-room, and the door close behind them.

Ten, twenty minutes, half an hour passed, still they did not come to her, though the sound of their merry laughter fell upon her ears from time to time. Katy tried to arouse her mistress' interest, but it was useless—the girl never moved from her position, sitting pale and white in the great arm-chair, with her sightless eyes turned toward the door.

Suddenly she turned to Katy with a great sob.

"They have forgotten me," she said.

Katy had come to this conclusion long before.

"I will tell them you are waiting," she replied, and as she spoke she hurried from the room to the drawing-room. On the threshold she came face to face with Mr. Kendal, and at a glance she could not help but notice the happy, flushed look on his face.

"Miss Dorothy sent me in search of you, sir," she said, with a low courtesy. The smile on his lips died away in an instant, giving place to a dark frown of impatience.

"What does she want?" he asked, sharply.

"She says she is so lonesome, sir, and sent me to tell you so."

"Is there a minute of my life that she is not sending for me—expecting me to be at her beck and call?" he said. "I am going out into the conservatory to get some flowers for Miss Vincent. I guess it won't hurt Dorothy to wait a little while, will it?"

"Is that what I shall tell her?" asked the girl, quietly.

"Tell her whatever you like," he said to the girl, hurrying on and leaving her standing there with a very white, sorrowful face.

Slowly she walked back to the breakfast-room, her heart burning with indignation. Dorothy met her eagerly.

"Are they coming?" she asked.

"Very soon now, miss," replied Katy.

"What delayed them?"

"I—I think they were getting a cup of tea for the strange young lady, miss. You know she came quite a long way, and she must be very tired."

"Why, that is very true," said Dorothy. "I wonder that I never thought of that before. It seemed as though I was not missed," and a sigh trembled over the girl's pale lips as she spoke.

A few moments later Kendal's step was heard in the corridor.

Dorothy sprang eagerly to meet him, and threw her arms impulsively around his neck.

Was it only her fancy, or did he draw back from the usual caress as though he did not care to receive it?

Oh! surely not. Since this horrible blindness had come upon her, her imagination was running riot against her judgment. The one great fear of her life was that he might cease to love her, now that this great affliction had come upon her, and she noted every word, every action, and every touch of his dear hand, and weighed it over in her mind, for hours at a time, when she found herself alone.

God pity her if that love should ever fail her!

"Shall Miss Vincent see me soon, Harry?" she asked, nestling her head against his shoulder, her little hands seeking his.

"Very soon now," he responded. Was it her fancy, or did even his voice seem changed?

"Do you like her?" asked Dorothy, wistfully.

"Like her?" he cried. "Why, she is charming!"

"Is she fair of face?" asked Dorothy, slowly.

"The most beautiful girl I have ever seen!" he cried, enthusiastically, all forgetful of the girl by his side, to whom his troth was plighted.

The words struck Dorothy's heart with a cold chill, as a blast of icy winter wind strikes death to the heart of a tender hot-house flower when its chill breath sweeps across it.

"They say you went down to the train to meet her," said Dorothy.

"Yes; Mrs. Kemp wanted me to," he responded; "and I shall never forget that meeting with her niece while life lasts, it was so ludicrous. I arrived at the depot just as the train had stopped, and the passengers were already pouring from the car. In my haste to reach the throng I slipped upon a banana peel, and the next instant I was plunging headlong forward, bumping straight into an old lady carrying numerous bundles and boxes, who had just alighted from the train.

"There was a crash and a yell, and a roar of laughter from the by-standers; and no wonder, for I had crashed directly into a huge jar of jam which she held in her hand, and in less time than it takes to tell it I was completely besmeared with it from head to foot. For once in my life I got enough jam in my mouth, and as I scrambled to my feet I beheld a young lady standing before me screaming with laughter.

"At a glance I knew it could be none other than Miss Vincent. What I said as I hastily stepped up to her is but a confused memory to me. I managed to articulate that I had been sent from Gray Gables with a carriage for her. The more I said the more she screamed with laughter, in which I could not help joining to have saved my life.

"'What! ride through the town with a jammed-up man like that!' she ejaculated. 'Why, that would be too sweet for anything—so sweet that all the bees in the clover fields we passed would come flying after us to enjoy the sport.'

"The laugh that followed fairly made the rafters of the old depot ring; and at this juncture a friend in need came to my assistance—one of my old chums—and in a trice had stripped off my coat and hat, and replaced them by a new overcoat and Derby hat which he had just purchased. And when the luckless jam was washed from my face 'Richard was himself again.'

"'Now you look something like a respectable human being,' she declared, as I helped her into the carriage.

"And all during the drive home we had the greatest kind of a laugh over my ludicrous mishap. It was forming each other's acquaintance under difficulties, as she phrased it. I can truthfully say that I never was so much embarrassed before a young girl in all my life. But do you know, Dorothy," he went on, "that that laughable incident which happened made us better acquainted with each other during that half hour's ride home than if we had met under ordinary circumstances and known each other for long months?"

Dorothy laughed heartily at the highly amusing scene which he pictured so graphically, and said to herself that now she could understand why Harry and this strange young girl were laughing so gayly together as they came up the graveled walk.

"You will be sure to like her," cried Harry, enthusiastically. "I will go and fetch her to you now."

But just as he was about to put his intention into execution, they heard the voice of Mrs. Kemp and her niece outside, and they entered an instant later.

"Dorothy," said Mrs. Kemp, "my niece, Iris, is here. Iris, this is Dorothy. I am sure you two girls will love each other dearly."

Dorothy, turned hastily toward the direction from whence the sound proceeded, holding out her little white hands nervously, a great hectic flush stealing up into her pale face.

"Welcome to Gray Gables, Miss Vincent—Iris," she said in her sweet, tremulous, girlish voice. "I—I would cross the room to where you are standing, if I could, but I can not. I can not look upon your face to welcome you, for—I am—blind!"

There was a *frou-frou* of skirts upon the velvet carpet, and the next moment Iris Vincent's arms were about her.

"There could not be a sweeter welcome, Dorothy—if I may call you so—and I am sure we shall get on famously together," murmured Miss Vincent, and a pair of ripe red lips met Dorothy's; but the kiss was as light as the brush of a butterfly's wings against the petals of a rose, and there was no warmth in the clasp of the soft, ringed fingers.

Somehow, although the stranger's voice was sweet as the sound of a silver lute, and her manner caressing, Dorothy did not feel quite at home with her.

"If I should judge by the tone of her voice and the words she utters, my fancy would lead me to believe that she was very beautiful," thought Dorothy. "But then Katy said that she was plain, very plain of face, although Harry has said that she was beautiful. No doubt he wanted to leave a good impression on my mind regarding her."

The evening that followed was a happy one for Dorothy, because, even without being coaxed, Harry signified his intention of remaining in the house, instead of going out to the club, as was his custom.

It had always been a deep grievance of Dorothy's that her musical accomplishments were so meager.

She only knew a few accompaniments that she had picked up, while Miss Vincent played divinely.

And her voice—ah! it sounded like the chiming of silver bells. And then, too, she knew so many beautiful songs, and they were all such tender love songs.

She was so glad that Harry liked them, too, and her poor face would flush scarlet, and her white lids droop over her sightless eyes, as the sweet singer's voice rose and thrilled over some tender love words; for she felt sure that her Harry was looking at her with all love's tender passion in his glorious dark eyes.

Chapter XI.

It was quite late when the group that was gathered in the drawing-room dispersed that evening; but when the girls found themselves alone in their own room, which they were to share together, they sat down for a comfortable chat ere they retired.

"Do you think you will like Gray Gables?" asked Dorothy.

"It seems pleasant enough," returned Iris, with a yawn; "but it's not the house so much, it's the people in the neighborhood. Are there many young folks hereabouts?"

"Quite a number."

"Are they very jolly, or are they terribly dull?"

"Well, about as jolly as Mr. Kendal," laughed Dorothy. "He's not so very jolly, and yet he is wonderfully good company."

"Yes, he is indeed," assented Miss Vincent. "Is he rich?" she asked, point-blank, in the very next breath.

"No," returned Dorothy; "but he may be well off some day, I hope."

"Handsome and poor! That's too bad—that's a poor combination!" sighed Miss Vincent, her countenance falling. "But tell me about him, Dorothy, and—and how he ever happened to take a fancy to a quiet little mouse like yourself. I have heard that it was your guardian's wish, as he was dying, and that the idea was quite a surprise to him—to Mr. Kendal, I mean. Is that true?"

"Yes," assented Dorothy, thoughtlessly enough.

She would not have answered the question in that way could she have seen the eager anxiety on the face of the girl who asked it.

"Does he make love to you very much?" whispered Iris, laying her soft cheek close against the blind girl's. "Forgive the question, but, do you know, I have always had a longing to know just what engaged people said to each other and how they acted—whether they grew more affectionate, or, after the grand climax of an engagement had been entered into, if—if somehow they did not act a little constrained toward each other."

Dorothy laughed long and merrily at the quaint ideas of her new friend. But, then, no doubt all girls wished to know that. She had done so herself once.

"You do not answer me," murmured Miss Vincent. "Now, please don't be unkind, Dorothy, when I'm just dying to know."

"Well," said Dorothy, waxing very confidential, after the fashion of girls, "I'll tell you *my* experience; but mind, I don't say that it is like every other girl's. Harry has been just a trifle bashful ever since the afternoon that he asked me to—to be his wife, and just a little constrained; but I always account for it in this way: that he does not want me to think him silly and spoony. He has grown, oh! ever so dignified. Why, he hardly ever says anything more about love—he thinks he has said all there is to say. And his caresses are the same way—just a little bit constrained, you know."

Iris Vincent had learned all she cared to know.

"Thank you, dear, ever so much, for gratifying my curiosity," she said aloud; but in her own heart she said:

"I knew it—I knew it! Handsome Harry Kendal does not love this girl with whom they have forced him into a betrothal. No wonder he looks sad and melancholy, with a prospect before him of marrying a blind wife! Ah, me! it is too dreadful a fate to even contemplate."

She looked complacently in the mirror at her own face. Well might Harry Kendal have remarked that it was as beautiful as a poet's dream.

Nothing could have been more exquisitely lovely than the deep, velvety, violet eyes, almost purple in their glorious depths, and the bronze-gold hair, such as Titian loved to paint, that fell in heavy curls to her slender waist.

One would scarcely meet in a life-time a girl of such wondrous loveliness. Iris was only twenty, but already she had broken hearts by the score.

She had only to smile at a man with those ripe, red, perfect lips, and give him one glance from those mesmeric eyes, and he was straightway her slave. And she gloried in her power.

Thrice she had broken up betrothals, and three young girls were heart-broken in consequence, and had lifted up their anguished voices and cursed her for her fatal beauty. But Iris only laughed her mellow, wicked little laugh when she heard of it, and said:

"Poor little simpletons! Before they engage themselves they ought to have been sure that they held their lovers' hearts completely. It were better for them to realize before than after marriage that the men they meant to stake their all upon could prove fickle at the first opportunity when a pretty girl crossed their paths."

And who could say that there was not some little truth in this?

The two girls whose paths were to cross so bitterly slept peacefully side by side that night; but long after Iris' eyes had closed in slumber, Dorothy lay awake with oh! such a heavy load on her heart.

She wished she was gay and bright, like Iris, and oh! what would she not have given only to see—only to see once again! And she turned her face to where she knew the moonlight lay in great yellow bars on the floor, and sobbed as she had never sobbed since she had become blind, and fell asleep with the tear-drops staining her pale face, a long, deep sigh trembling over her lips.

Both girls awoke early the next morning.

"When do you have breakfast?" asked Iris, with a yawn.

"At eight o'clock," said Dorothy; "so we need not be in a hurry about getting up. It can not be more than six now."

"Oh, dear! then I shall have to get up at once," cried Iris; "for it takes me fully that long to dress."

"Two hours!" cried Dorothy, amazed, adding: "Why, just put on a wrapper. Nobody here ever thinks of making a toilet to appear at the breakfast-table. There is no one but Mrs. Kemp, Harry, you and I."

She could not catch Iris' unintelligible reply, but she noticed that the girl was not to be persuaded.

She commenced dressing at once.

Soon Dorothy detected a strange odor of burning paper in the room.

"What is that?" she cried, in alarm. "Oh, Miss Vincent, the house must be on fire!"

Iris laughed long and loud.

"You delightful, innocent little goose!" she cried. "I am only curling my bangs with an iron heated over the gas, and I'm trying the tongs on paper to see that they are not too hot. I put my curls up in paper last night, but the horrid old things wouldn't curl because of the damp atmosphere, and—" She did not finish the sentence for Dorothy supplied it in her own mind—"her new friend was desirous of looking her best."

Harry was pacing impatiently up and down the breakfast-room when they entered.

"Good-morning, Miss Vincent; good-morning, Dorothy!" he exclaimed, eagerly; and Dorothy's heart gave a quick start, noting that he called her name last.

And another thing struck Dorothy quite forcibly. To her great surprise, she noticed that Iris spoke in quite a different tone from what she did when they were alone together in their own room.

There her accents were drawling, but now they were so wonderfully sweet and musical that Dorothy was struck with wonder. She never knew that a person could speak in two different tones of voice like this.

At the breakfast-table the conversation was bright and merry, though outside the rain had commenced to patter against the window-pane.

Dorothy felt strangely diffident, for only a small portion of the conversation was directed now and then to her, and Harry and Miss Vincent kept up such a lively chatter that there was scarcely an opportunity to get in a word edgewise.

The conversation turned upon horseback riding, and it brought a strange pang to Dorothy's heart, for that had been the most pleasurable accomplishment she had learned during the first few weeks she had been at Gray Gables, and she loved it passionately.

In the very hour when they told her that she would for evermore be blind—stone-blind—the cry that had sprung to her lips was, "And can I never again ride Black Beauty?" and she bowed her head in a storm of wild and tempestuous grief.

For many a day after Harry would not even have the name of Black Beauty mentioned in her hearing. And now how strange that he should bring up the subject in her presence!

"I am sorry it is raining, Miss Vincent," he said, "for I had promised myself such a pleasure for this morning. I had intended asking you to join me in a canter over the country. This is just the season of the year to enjoy the bracing air. We have a little horse in the stable that would delight you, if you are a judge of equine flesh. Its very name indicates what it is—Black Beauty. You ride, of course?"—this interrogatively.

"Oh, yes!" declared Iris; "and I always thought it would be the height of my ambition if I could own a horse."

"That would be a very slight ambition to gratify," returned Harry Kendal. "You may have—"

He was about to add, "Black Beauty," but at that instant his eyes fell upon Dorothy. She was leaning forward, her sightless eyes turned in his direction, with a world of anguish in them that would have melted a heart of stone.

Mrs. Kemp saw the storm approaching, and said, hastily:

"I have always been thinking of buying a pony for my niece, and if she is a very good girl, she may get one for Christmas."

Harry looked his thanks to Mrs. Kemp for coming to his rescue so timely.

Dorothy lingered after the others had left the breakfast-room, and called to Harry to wait a minute, as she wished to speak with him.

He had a guilty conscience; he knew what was coming. She meant to ask him if he intended offering Black Beauty to Miss Vincent, and, of course, he made up his mind to deny it.

Chapter XII.

The long weeks that had passed since the never-to-be-forgotten steamboat incident on Labor Day passed like a nightmare to poor Jack Garner.

Slowly but surely the knowledge had come to him that Dorothy, his little sweetheart, had faded like a dream from his life; and as this became a settled fact in his mind, his whole nature seemed to change.

He grew reckless, morbid, and gay by turns, until his old mother grew terrified, fearing for his reason. His whole heart had been in his work before and his one aim in life had been to make money.

He had saved quite a snug little sum, which he very prudently placed in the bank.

Now, to his mother's horror, his recklessness lost him his position, and he did not have enough ambition to try and secure another place, but commenced to draw his little hoard from the bank, and his money was disappearing like snow before a summer's sun.

He began coming in late at nights, as well, and the widow, who listened for his footsteps, cried out in anguish: "Would to God that I had died ere I had lived to see this horrible change take place in my idolized son!"

His cousin Barbara keenly felt the change in him. It was she who comforted the poor old mother, and who pleaded with Jack to try and take up the duties of life again, and to forget faithless Dorothy.

But he would only shake his head, and answer that he would never cease to love Dorothy and search for her while life lasted. But troubles never seem to come singly. One day, as Jack was pacing restlessly up and down Broadway—the vantage-ground which he always sought at six o'clock each evening, to scan the faces of the working-girls as they passed, with the lingering hope in his heart that some day, sooner or later, his vigilance would be rewarded by seeing Dorothy—a terrible accident happened which almost cost him his life.

An old sign on one of the corner buildings, which had done service many a year, suddenly fell, and Jack—poor Jack, was knocked senseless to the pavement.

Surely it was the workings of Providence that Jessie Staples happened along just at that critical moment.

With a wild, bitter cry she sprang forward, flinging herself upon the prostrate body, shrieking out as she saw his handsome, white face with the stains of blood upon it:

"Oh, Heaven have mercy! It is Jack—Jack Garner!"

Kindly hands raised him. No, he was not dead—only stunned, and terribly bruised.

A cab was hastily summoned, and, accompanied by Jessie, he was taken home.

The girl broke the sad news gently to Jack's mother and to Barbara. It was many and many a day before Jack left his couch; the accident had proved more dangerous than had been at first anticipated, for brain fever had set in.

Every day on her way home from the book-bindery Jessie would go several blocks out of her way to see how Jack was getting along, and Barbara and his mother soon discovered that it was something more than mere friendship that actuated the girl's visits. Although against their expostulations, every cent that she could scrape together, over and above the cost of the bare necessities of her living, she would expend for fruit to bring to Jack.

"I feel such a great pity for him," she would say; "for he has never, never been the same since Dorothy disappeared so suddenly." And they would look at the girl with wistful eyes, realizing that in her case, surely, pity was akin to love.

They guessed Jessie's secret long before she knew it herself, and they felt sorry for her; for they knew her hopes were useless—that Jack could never return the girl's love.

Jack's mother and Barbara talked the matter over carefully, and concluded that it was best for the girl's peace of mind to break up this infatuation, if they could, at once.

At this epoch an event happened which turned the tide of affairs into a strange channel.

By the death of a relative Jack suddenly found himself possessed of a fortune.

He heard the startling news with a white, calm, unmoved face, while his mother and Barbara almost went wild with joy over it.

"It matters little to me now," he said. "Wealth has no charms for me." And they well knew why.

The intelligence came like a thunderbolt to Jessie Staples.

It was Mrs. Garner who told about it while the family were gathered about the tea-table.

The girl's face grew white as death, and she looked over at Jack with startled eyes.

Before she could ask the question that sprang to her lips, Mrs. Garner added:

"Of course this will make a great change in Jack's prospects. He says that we shall soon leave the little cottage and go out West somewhere—Barbara and I and himself—and that we will leave New York City far behind us, as there is no tie that binds him here now."

Jessie tried to speak, but the words refused to come to her icy lips. She made an effort to raise her eyes to Jack's face, with a careless smile; but it was a failure—a dire failure.

The table seemed to suddenly rise and dance before her.

She rose hastily, with a wild prayer that she might get quickly out of the room, for she felt her throat choking up with great sobs, and realized that in an instant more she would have burst into tears.

Poor Jessie Staples took one step forward, then fell unconscious at Jack's feet.

"Why, what in the world can be the matter with Jessie?" he cried, raising her in his strong arms. "Is she ill? Let us send for a physician—quick!"

"Stay!" said his mother, as he deposited Jessie on the sofa and turned quickly to put this last thought into execution. "Jessie's trouble is one which no physician can alleviate. It is an affair of the heart."

Jack looked at his mother in amazement.

"An affair of the heart?" he repeated. "Surely not, mother. Why, I have known Jessie ever since I can remember, and I never knew her to have a beau."

"Perhaps she has given her heart to some one who does not return her love—who may not even know of it," suggested Mrs. Garner, quietly.

"Impossible," declared Jack. "I have known her for years, I say, and if there was an affair of the heart between Jessie and any of the young men at the bindery, I should have known something of it."

Mrs. Garner came nearer and laid her hand on her son's arm.

"Are you *sure*, Jack?" she asked, in a low voice.

He gave a great start.

"I know of one whom she loves, and who, she knows, never thinks of her. When his life hung in jeopardy her secret was revealed to me."

"Surely you *do not*—you *can not* mean, mother—that she—that I—"

"Yes, that is what I mean," returned Mrs. Garner, quietly. "Jessie Staples loves *you*, my boy; but do not be hard on the poor girl. Remember, love goes where it is sent. She never intended that you should know it. She did not breathe a word about it to any one. It was by the merest chance that we made the discovery, and she does not dream that we know it."

Jack sank down in the nearest chair, quite overcome with dismay.

His mother came and bent over him, smoothing the fair hair back from his damp brow with a trembling hand, but uttering no word.

At last he broke the deep silence:

"What am I to say—what am I to do, mother, if—if—your surmises be actually true?"

"They are not surmises, my boy," returned his mother; "they are truths."

"You know that I like Jessie," he went on, huskily; "but as for any other sentiment—why, it would be impossible. My life will always be tinged with the bitter sorrow of that other love-dream which was so cruelly shattered. I—I wish to Heaven you had not told me your suspicions about Jessie, mother."

"Her secret fell from my lips in an unguarded moment," she answered, slowly, "and I am sorry you know all. Yet it must be a source of comfort to you to know that although Dorothy Glenn was false to you, there is *one* heart which beats only for you."

Jack started to his feet, a dull pallor creeping into his face as he drew back from his mother's touch.

"Dorothy is *not false* to me!" he cried. "If an angel from heaven should tell me so I would not believe it. She is my betrothed bride. She wears my betrothal-ring upon her little hand. No matter where she is, she is true to me—true as God's promise. Shame has caused her to hide herself from me, because she was so foolish as to go with another on an excursion on Labor Day. But I have forgiven all that long ago. Oh, Heaven! if I could but let her know it!"

Mrs. Garner shook her head.

"A young girl who can leave you for months without a word does not care for you, my boy," she answered, sadly. "Surely there is great truth in the words that 'Love is blind,' if you can not be made to see this."

Still the noble lover shook his head. There was no power on earth strong enough to shake his faith in Dorothy's love.

Mrs. Garner had said all that she could say for Jessie, and she bowed her head, and great tears rolled down her cheeks. She felt great pity for Jessie. Why could not her son love her? She had heard the story of jilted lovers turning to some sympathizing heart for solace, and in time learning to love their consoler, and she wondered if this might not mercifully happen to her darling, idolized boy.

She watched him as he paced excitedly up and down the room. Suddenly he turned to her, and during all the long after years of sorrow and pain she never forgot the expression of his face.

"Mother!" he cried, hoarsely, "if my Dorothy ever proved false to me, I should be tempted to—to—kill her—and—then—kill—myself!"

CHAPTER XIII.

The *contretemps* which had been so cleverly averted—of giving the pony, Black Beauty, to Miss Vincent, and Dorothy's keen resentment—should have proved a lesson to Harry Kendal and warned him not to play with edged tools.

He was a little careful of what he said to Iris for the next few days, when Dorothy was present; but gradually this restraint began to wear off, and he grew to be almost reckless in the way he laughed and carried on with the girl, even though his *fiancée* was in the room. This attention was certainly not discouraged by Iris Vincent.

He smiled to see her go in raptures over everything in and about Gray Gables, and she, with her glorious dark eyes, always smiled back at him. Their chats grew longer and more frequent; they were fast becoming excellent friends.

They had sent for Iris Vincent to become Dorothy's companion, but it was whispered among the old servants of the household that she was proving herself to be more frequently the companion of Mr. Kendal, and they talked about it in alarm, wondering how it would all end. They felt indignant, too, that such a bold flirtation—for it had certainly come to that—should be carried on right in the face of poor, blind Dorothy.

"Some one ought to give her a hint of what is going on," cried indignant little Katy, the maid. But there was no one who could find it in his or her heart to warn her of what was transpiring. The blow would be more than she could bear, for she loved Harry Kendal better than life itself.

They wondered if little Dorothy guessed that he led Iris to the table, while she, blind as she was, groped her way as best she could to her own seat. They hated to see him lavish attentions on the beauty, and it drove them almost out of their self-possession to see their eyes meet in that provoking, mutual smile.

Dorothy was beginning to feel Harry's neglect, but no thought of the true cause of it ever dawned upon her.

Ah! could she have seen how they paced the grounds together arm in arm, and how near they sat together on the step of the front porch, and in what a lover-like manner he bent his dark head over her little, white hands, the sight would have killed Dorothy.

"I wonder if they think we are fools!" whispered the servants, indignantly, one to the other; and their blood boiled with rage at this open love-making.

But even the attention of handsome Harry Kendal seemed to pall upon the beauty. Gray Gables was dull; she wanted more life, more gayety.

"Why not give a grand ball," she suggested, "and invite the whole country-side?"

She longed for more hearts to conquer. Iris was one of those vain, shallow girls who must and will have a sentimental flirtation with some young man always on hand. She, like those of her mischievous class, really meant no harm while doing a great deal of wrong. Such a girl, from mere vanity and pastime, will try to outshine a companion and even win the heart of a betrothed lover from his sweetheart, caring little for the broken vows and the ruined lives strewn along her path.

Harry Kendal seized eagerly upon the idea, because it would please Iris. Mrs. Kemp knew no other than her beautiful, willful niece's pleasure. No one consulted Dorothy. She seemed to have been left entirely out of the calculation.

For the first time since Iris Vincent had come to Gray Gables, Dorothy regretted her presence there.

What would be the ball to her? Surely they ought to know that she could take no part in it, for she was blind.

When she found herself alone with Iris she spoke of this, but the girl turned it off with a little laugh.

"Even so," she declared, "Gray Gables ought not to be shut up and barricaded. You need to have a little life to keep your spirits up. You are just dying for some kind of liveliness. And poor Harry! every one is feeling sorry for him. They say he is growing so dull."

"Do they say that?" cried Dorothy, the color deepening in her cheeks.

"Yes—and more," assented Iris. "And for that reason I would advise you to study appearances, so that every one may know that he is happy—at least, let them think he is."

The words struck Dorothy with a cold chill, as her companion had intended that they should.

"Then let the ball be given, by all means," returned Dorothy, with a little quiver in her voice.

And so the matter was arranged.

For the next week Iris and Harry were busy with the invitations. They sat side by side, comparing them as they made them out, and never once seemed to note Dorothy's presence.

If any one on the list did not quite suit their fancy, they were quickly rejected; but Dorothy noticed that he never once turned to her, his betrothed bride, and asked her opinion.

There was one young girl to whom Dorothy had been quite attached, who lived very near Gray Gables, and who had run over to see her almost every day, up to the time Iris had come. Since then her visits had been less and less frequent; within the last fortnight they had ceased altogether.

Dorothy was very anxious, of course, that this young girl should be invited; but Iris put in a demurrer at once.

"Of all the girls I ever met, I dislike her the most," declared Iris.

She was very careful not to tell the real reason why.

This same young girl had been the first to notice her flirtation with Harry Kendal. They had had quite a stormy little scene over it, for the girl had attempted to rebuke Iris, in her modest way, and she had retorted by flashing out that it was none of her business, anyway, saying that she would flirt with Harry Kendal just as much as she pleased, and that it was a shame for such a handsome young fellow to marry a girl stone blind.

They had parted in anger. No wonder, we repeat, that Iris objected to inviting Dorothy's friend to the grand ball.

"Oh! of course we must invite her," said Dorothy, when her friend's name was brought under discussion. "Mustn't we, Harry?"

He turned away and walked moodily to the window without replying. If Iris did not like her, that settled the matter. He dared not put in one word in the girl's favor, though Dorothy was clamoring for his opinion.

"You must settle the matter, Harry," said Dorothy.

"Let me suggest a better way," he replied, gallantly, as he took his seat at the table again. "You two girls arrange it between yourselves."

"But we do not think we will come to an agreement," pouted Iris. "You will have to choose for Dorothy and me."

He gave her a startled, sweeping look, and she knew by that that he would not dare go against her for Dorothy.

"I must decline," he said again, for he felt nervous with those sightless eyes turned eagerly in his direction.

"You must say 'Yes' or 'No,'" said Dorothy, never dreaming that his answer would be in the negative, for on the week that she had first come to Gray Gables he had said: "I must introduce you at once to Alice Lee, who lives across the way. She is a lovely, quiet girl, and I know you will like her." And Dorothy had liked gentle Alice Lee.

She thought of this now as the question of inviting her to the ball had come up, and never for a moment had she doubted the result of his decision.

"You must answer 'Yes' or 'No,'" pouted Iris, impatiently. "Come, we are wasting time."

Iris leaned over close to his chair—so near that the dark rings of her hair brushed his cheek, thrilling him to the soul.

"You must choose," she whispered; and he knew that it was a challenge as to which he should please—herself or Dorothy.

Closer, closer still she leaned, until his very pulses grew mad with the nearness of her presence, and with child-like confidence her soft little hand crept into his, and nestled there securely.

There was no one to see, though Dorothy—God help her!—sat so near her. The touch of that little hand was magical. In the mad impulse of the moment he raised it to his lips and kissed it, and Iris knew that she had won the battle even before he spoke.

"Alice Lee had better not be invited to the ball," he said, huskily. "That is my decision."

Dorothy sank back in her chair as though a sudden blow had been struck her. She never once dreamed that her betrothed lover would decide against her.

It fairly took her breath away, and a sudden new sensation shot through her heart that had never found lodgment there before.

She drew back and said no more, a deathly pallor overspreading her face. She did not interfere again, and she suffered them to arrange the invitations after that to please themselves.

She rose quietly at length and made her way to the window, great tears rising to her sightless eyes.

They did not even notice her absence, but chatted and laughed quite the same.

After they had finished Harry proposed that they should take the invitations to be mailed. This Iris gayly assented to, and they left the room without once making any excuse to Dorothy for leaving her there alone.

The fact was that they were not even aware that she had seated herself in the bay window behind the great, heavy *portières*.

For the first time Dorothy wished that Iris had not come. She was already beginning to feel the weight of the iron hand that was soon to crush her—jealousy.

She awaited their coming with the greatest impatience, but it was long hours ere they returned.

Chapter XIV.

Harry Kendal did not intend being untrue to Dorothy when he let himself drift into that platonic friendship with Iris, the beauty, which had developed into such a dangerous flirtation.

Gradually the girl's fascinations seemed to overpower him, and before he quite realized it, Iris had become part and parcel of his life.

On the way to the postoffice a little event had happened which had almost changed the current of his life.

They had taken the short cut from Gray Gables to the postoffice, which lay over the hills, and were walking along arm in arm when suddenly Iris' foot slipped upon a stone, and she stumbled headlong in the path with a little, terrified cry.

In an instant Harry had raised her, and to his utter consternation she clung to him half fainting.

"Oh, Mr. Kendal—Harry—I—I have sprained my ankle! I can not walk!" she said; and a low cry of pain broke from her lips.

He gathered her close in his arms, and did everything in his power to soothe her.

"I am so sorry—so sorry that I let you undertake this trip with me. Let me carry you back to the house."

"My—my ankle is not sprained," she faltered; "it was only wrenched a little as it turned over against that stone. We will sit down on this log a few moments, and after a little rest I will be all right again."

To this Kendal willingly assented, but he did not remove his arm from the slender waist.

"I am so thankful that it is no worse, Iris," he breathed, huskily.

"Would you have cared so very much if I had sprained my ankle?" she faltered, looking up into his face with those great, dark, mesmeric eyes that no one had ever yet been able to resist.

He looked away from her quickly and did not reply.

"Would you?" persisted Iris, in her low, musical voice.

Throwing prudence to the winds, he turned to her suddenly and clasped her still closer in his arms.

"Does not your own heart teach you that, Iris?" he returned, hoarsely.

"Oh! if I could only believe what my heart would fain tell me," she murmured, "I—I would be so happy!"

"If it told you that I—I love you," he cried, "then it would—"

The rest of the sentence died away on his lips for there, directly in the path before him, stood Mrs. Kemp. She might have been blind to all her beautiful niece's short-comings, but she was not a woman to so mix right and wrong as to permit Iris to listen to a word of love from one she knew belonged, in the sight of God, to another.

Iris was equal to the occasion.

"Oh, aunt!" she cried, "I am so glad that you happened along just now. I—I hurt my foot, and it was so painful that I had to sit down and rest; and Mr. Kendal was kind enough to remain here with me a few moments, although—although—besides the invitations we had to mail, he had other important letters to go out to-day."

"Are you quite sure your ankle is not sprained, my dear?" cried Mrs. Kemp, in alarm. "The wisest thing to do will be to come home with me at once, and we will send for a doctor to examine it."

Iris sprang to her feet with a wicked little laugh.

"See, it is better now—almost as good as new," she declared, "thanks to Mr. Kendal for insisting upon my sitting down here to rest."

Had it been any one else but Iris, Kendal would have said the affair had been a clever little ruse to give him the opportunity to make love to her.

But in this instance it never occurred to him but that Iris was telling the plain facts—that her ankle had been wrenched, and with a few moments' rest it was as good as ever again.

Mrs. Kemp looked greatly relieved.

"We may as well be going," said Iris, hoping that her aunt would pass on and leave them to enjoy the *téte-à-téte* which she had interrupted at such an inopportune time.

"I will go with you both as far as the postoffice," said Mrs. Kemp; and the good soul did not notice the expression of annoyance on both faces, and, very much against the will of each, she accompanied them there and back.

Iris was bitterly annoyed, but she was diplomatic enough to conceal it; and she could see, too, by Harry's face that he was disappointed in being so ruthlessly cheated out of a *téte-à-téte* with her.

They loitered long by the way, trusting that Mrs. Kemp would become impatient with their delay, and excuse herself, to get back to the house in time to superintend dinner, which was quite a feature at Gray Gables.

"You do not seem to be in any hurry to-day," laughed Iris, eyeing her aunt sideways.

"No; for it is not often that I indulge myself in going out for a stroll," answered Mrs. Kemp, "and I need to make the most of it. If I am not back at the usual time Dorothy will superintend affairs—bless her dear little heart! Why, she's a regular little jewel about the house, even with her affliction."

This praise of Dorothy was anything but pleasant to Iris, especially when Kendal was present, and she turned the conversation at once into another channel.

As they neared the house they met one of the servants hurrying down the road.

"You are the very person I am looking for, ma'am," he cried, breathlessly. "There is something the matter with the range, and they are all in a stew over it, not knowing what to do until you come."

"Good gracious! if I step out of the house for a moment something is sure to happen," cried the good old lady, despairingly. "Say that I will be there directly, John;" and much to Iris' relief, she hurriedly left them.

"Why need we hasten?" said Kendal, in a low voice. "This is the pleasantest part of the afternoon."

"I am in no hurry," assented the girl.

"We will linger here in this delightful spot, and I will gather you some autumn leaves," cried Harry. "Would you like that?"

"Yes," she assented; "if you will help me to weave them into garlands."

"Nothing would give me more pleasure," he declared; "that is, if you are not afraid of the old tradition becoming true."

She looked up into his face, blushing as crimson as the heart of a deep-red rose.

"I have never heard it," she said. "Do tell me what it is."

"Bye and bye, with your permission, while we are weaving the garlands," Harry answered, with a rich, mellow laugh. "If I should tell you beforehand, you might refuse to accept my services altogether."

"Is it so bad as that?" laughed Iris.

"You had better use the word *good* instead of bad. The idea would be more pleasant."

"Not knowing what you are talking about, and not possessing the key to solve the riddle of your incomprehensible words, I had better make no further reply, lest I get into deep water," she pouted. "But really you have aroused my curiosity."

"Well, when we have the first wreath made, then, and not until then, will I tell you what they say of the youth and maiden who weave autumn leaves for each other, and together. Come and sit on this mossy ledge. I will spread my overcoat upon it. It shall be your throne."

"I will be a queen, but where will be my king?" laughed Iris, gayly.

"Your king will come a-wooing all in good time," he answered, his dark eyes seeking hers with a meaning glance, which the beauty and coquette understood but too well.

In less time than it takes to tell it, Kendal had gathered about her heaps of the beautiful, shining leaves.

"Oh, aren't they lovely!" cried Iris, delightedly. "I fairly adore autumn leaves."

"I did not know that you had such an eye for the beautiful in nature," he retorted, rather pleased.

"I adore everything that is handsome," she said, in a low voice, returning his look of a few moments ago with interest.

An hour flew by on golden wings, and the wreaths grew beneath their touch.

"Now you look indeed a queen!" cried Harry, raising one gracefully, and laying it on the girl's dark curls. "You remind me just now of pictures I have seen of Undine and the woodland nymphs."

"Ah! but Undine had no heart," declared Iris.

"In some respects you are like Undine," he retorted. "She never knew she had a heart till she was conscious of its loss. Ah, but you do look bewitching, Miss Vincent—Iris, with that wreath of autumn foliage on your head, like a crown of dying sunset. When I see the leaves turn in the autumn, lines that I read somewhere always recur to me:

"'As bathed in blood the trailing vines appear,While 'round them, soft and low, the wild wind grieves;The heart of autumn must have broken here,And poured her treasure out upon the leaves.'"

"What pretty poetry!" sighed Iris. "Why, it seems to me that you have some beautiful sentiment, set to rhyme, to express almost every thought! You must love poetry. Does—does Dorothy care for it?"

"No," he returned, in a low voice, and looked away from her with a moody brow.

"That is strange," mused Iris. "I should think that you would inspire her with a love for it."

"If it is not in one's soul, how can you expect to find it there," he retorted, rather bitterly. "No, Dorothy has no love for poetry, flowers, or birds, nor, in fact, anything that other young girls care for. I imagine she would quite as soon prefer a garden filled with hollyhocks and morning-glories to the daintiest flowers that ever bloomed. Alas, there are few tastes in common between us!"

CHAPTER XV.

"What a pity!" sighed Iris, and her hand crept sympathizingly into his. The gloomy look deepened on his face.

"Do you believe that there is a true mate for each heart, Iris?" he asked, suddenly.

"I might better ask *you* that question," she answered, evasively. "You are engaged—*you* seem to have found a heart that is the mate for your own."

"Do you think there is such a thing as making a mistake, even in so grave a matter?" he asked, huskily, "and that those who discover their error should keep on straying further and further in the wrong path? Do you not believe that there should be the most ardent love between those who wed—and that where there is a lack of it the two should separate, and each go his or her own way?"

Iris drooped her head; but ere she could reply—utter the words that sprang to her lips—an exclamation of the deepest annoyance, mingled with a fierce imprecation, was ground out from between Kendal's teeth.

There, directly in the path before them, stood Alice Lee.

Had she been standing there long? If so, she must have heard every word that had been uttered.

Alice Lee had heard, and every word had cut to her heart like the sharp point of a sword.

She had feared this, but had tried to reason the matter out in her own mind; but although circumstances did look tellingly against the beauty who had come to Gray Gables to be Dorothy Glenn's companion, yet she had tried to make herself believe that her suspicions were groundless.

"Have you been eavesdropping?" cried Iris, springing to her feet, her black eyes flashing luridly.

A thousand thoughts flashed through Alice Lee's mind in an instant.

No; she was too proud to let them realize that she had overheard the perfidy of Dorothy's treacherous lover.

No; better plead ignorance, until she had time to think over the matter, for Dorothy's sake, if not for her own.

"I have but just turned the bend in the road," she replied, with sweet girlish dignity. "Your question, Miss Vincent, surprises me," she said. "I have no need to answer it, I think."

"But you always do happen around just when people least expect you, Alice Lee."

"I hope my old friends will always find my presence welcome," returned Alice, quietly.

"To be sure, you are welcome," interposed Kendal. "Miss Vincent and I were only conversing upon the salient points of a new novel we finished reading yesterday. If you would care to hear it, I shall be pleased to go over the plot with you, and hear your opinion regarding it."

"I fear it would not benefit you, for I am not much of a novel reader, and understand very little of plots and plotting."

Was this a quiet drive at them? both thought as they looked up instantly.

But the soft, gray eyes of Alice Lee looked innocently enough from one to the other.

She seemed in no hurry to pass on, and Iris felt that for the second time that afternoon her *téte-à-téte* with handsome Harry Kendal was to be broken up, and from this moment henceforth she owed Alice Lee more of a grudge than ever, and she felt sure that the girl knew it.

Upon one point Alice was determined—that no matter how coldly Iris Vincent might treat her, she should not leave Dorothy's lover alone with her and in her power—she would stand by her poor little blind friend, who needed her aid in this terrible hour more than she would ever know, God help her!

Although long silences fell between the trio, still Alice lingered, chatting so innocently that they could not find it in their hearts to be very angry with her; and they could not bring themselves to believe that she had a purpose in her guileless actions.

There was no alternative but to walk homeward with her; but they did not ask her in when they reached the gates of Gray Gables, and so Alice had no excuse to enter to see Dorothy and warn her, but was obliged to pass on.

Mrs. Kemp and two or three of the servants were on the porch, so that there was no opportunity to exchange but a few whispered words. They were just about to part when Iris happened to think that Kendal had not told her what was said of those who gather and weave autumn leaves together, as he had promised.

She paused suddenly and looked up archly into his face.

"What about the autumn-leaf mystery?" she exclaimed. "You know you were to tell me all about it?"

"Do you promise not to be angry with me, Iris?" he answered, in his deep, musical voice. "You know I can not help old adages—I do not make them."

"Why should I be angry?" she exclaimed, having a rather faint idea of what was coming.

"Well, then," said Kendal, fixing his dark eyes full upon her, "it is said that the youth and maiden who twine the ruby and golden leaves together are intended for each other. There, are you so very angry?"

Iris dropped his arm with a little cry, and fled precipitately into the house.

He walked on slowly through the great hall and into the library. He knew Dorothy would be waiting for him, and he did not feel equal to the ordeal of meeting her just then.

He wanted a moment to think. He felt that he was standing on the brink of a fearful abyss, and that one more step must prove fatal to him.

Which way should he turn? He was standing face to face with the terrible truth now, that he loved Iris Vincent madly—loved her better than his own life—he, the betrothed of another.

But with that knowledge came another. Iris could be nothing to him, for they were both poor.

He was sensible enough to sit down and look the future in the face. He realized that if he should marry Iris on the spur of the moment, that would be only the beginning of the end.

It would be all gay and bright with them for a few brief weeks, or perhaps for a few months; then their sky would change, for Iris was not a girl to endure poverty for love's sake. She wanted the luxuries of life—these he could not give her; and there would be reproaches from the lips that now had only smiles for him.

She would want diamonds and silks, and all the other feminine extravagances so dear to the hearts of other women, and he was only a struggling doctor, who would have to fight a hand-to-hand battle with grim poverty. And sitting there in the arm-chair, before the glowing grate, where he had flung himself, he pictured a life of poverty that would spread out before him if he defied the world for love's sake.

A dingy office; a worn coat, and trousers shiny at the knees; a necktie with a ragged edge; an unkempt beard, a last season's hat, and hunger gnawing at his vitals.

The picture filled him with the most abject horror.

He was stylish and fastidious to a fault. He loved Iris; but did he not equally love his own ease? He could barely tolerate Dorothy, the poor, tender, plain little creature who lavished a world of love upon him; but he swallowed the bitter draught of having to endure her by always remembering that she was heiress, in all probability, to a cool million of money, and money had been his idol all his life long. He could not exist without it.

He was not one of the kind who could face the world manfully and snatch from it its treasures by the sweat of his brow. No, he could not give up this dream of wealth that was almost as much as life to him.

In the very midst of his reverie a light step crossed the library, but he did not hear it. It was Dorothy.

She stole up quietly and knelt on the hassock beside his chair.

"What were you thinking of, Harry?" she said.

He was equal to the occasion.

"Of what or whom should I be thinking but yourself, Dorothy?" he replied.

"It could not have been a very pleasant thought, I fear, for you sighed deeply," she murmured.

"That is all your fancy, Dorothy," he declared—"that my thoughts were not pleasant. True, I may have sighed, but did you never hear of such a thing as a sigh of contentment?"

She laughed merrily.

"I have heard of it, but thought the words rather misplaced."

"I assure you they are quite true and practicable."

"Where is Iris?" she asked, suddenly.

"I am sure I do not know," he answered, trying to speak carelessly.

"I want to have a real long talk with you, Harry," she said. "I have heard that there should be nothing but the utmost confidence between engaged lovers. Shall it not be so with us?"

"Of course," he answered, starting rather guiltily, for he had a faint intuition of what was coming.

"Harry," she whispered, "I want you to tell me—is it true—what they are all saying—that you have ceased to love me?"

"All saying!" he echoed. "Who is saying it? What old busybodies are sticking their noses in my affairs now?" he cried, with something on his lips that sounded very like an imprecation.

"But it isn't true, is it, Harry?" she breathed. "I should want to die if I thought it was."

"Look here, Dorothy," he cried, "if you want to believe all these mischief-makers tell you, you will have enough to do all through your life. You will have to either believe me or believe them. Now, which shall it be?"

"But answer my question, 'Yes' or 'No?'" pleaded Dorothy. "I—I am waiting for your answer, Harry."

There was a slight rustle in the doorway, and glancing up with a start, Kendal saw Iris Vincent standing there, looking on the tender scene with a scornful smile, and the words he would have answered died away unsaid on his lips.

Chapter XVI.

With a scornful toss of her head, Iris wheeled about. She would not enter the room, though she was just dying to know what they were saying—as Kendal sat in the arm-chair before the glowing coals, while Dorothy knelt on the hassock at his feet.

But that one glance of Iris had proved fatal to Kendal's peace of mind, and the hope swept over his soul that she would not think that he was talking love to Dorothy.

His silence perplexed the girl kneeling at his feet.

"I try to picture what our future life will be together, Harry," she murmured.

"Don't let us talk about it!" he exclaimed, impatiently.

"But I like to," she insisted. "It is my constant thought by night and by day. And, oh! I shall try to make you so happy. I shall go out dining with you every day, if you like, and I will always wear a little veil over my face, that no one need know as they pass us by that your bride is blind. And I shall try to be so wise, and learn to talk with you upon the subjects you love best. You will not be ashamed of me, will you, Harry?"

This with wistful eagerness pitiful to behold.

"I do wish, Dorothy, that you would cease your harping on the same old subject!" he cried, worriedly. "You annoy me so!"

"Annoy you?" whispered Dorothy, half under her breath. "Why, I did not know that we could say anything to those we love which could make them vexed at us, because I thought we were:

"'Two souls with but a single thought, Two hearts that beat as one.'

It seems, Harry, as though we had so little time to talk with each other now. And, oh! how I miss those little chats we used to have together; don't you?"

"You talk like a child, Dorothy," he cried. "Do you expect me to be dancing attendance upon you all the time?"

"No; I have ceased to expect that," murmured the girl, choking back a sob—"especially lately."

"I hope," he cried, "that you are not getting to be one of those exacting creatures who are jealous if a man is not at their side every moment? I could never endure that."

With a sudden impulse, Dorothy threw her arms about his neck and nestled her snow-white cheek against his.

"Let me tell you the truth, Harry," she whispered. "I am trying not to be jealous, as hard as ever I can; but, oh! there seems such a coldness between us lately. My intuition—my heart tells me so. Everything has changed since Iris came," she repeated. "I am glad you have some one to go with you on your rambles, as I used to do—some one to walk and read with you, as I once did. But when I think of it, and picture you two together, and know that she takes the same place by your side that I was wont to take, can you wonder that my heart throbs with a slow, dull pain?"

"Women magnify everything!" cried Kendal, harshly. "I suppose you will begrudge me a moment's comfort where another young girl is concerned, because you can not participate in it."

"I wonder that you can find comfort, as you phrase it, with another," said Dorothy, with a little tremor in her voice. "I have never heard that any other society was satisfying to an engaged lover than that of the sweetheart whom he avers to love."

Kendal laughed a little low, tantalizing laugh which grated keenly on the girl's ears.

"Men differ in their tastes and inclinations," he retorted laconically. "I do not choose to be tied down and governed by one woman's whims, nor to be dictated to."

"You should not speak of it in that way, Harry," whispered the girl in a choking voice; "rather, you should say to yourself that you would not do the slightest thing that might cause me one pang of annoyance. He who truly loves finds no interest, no attraction but in the one face, the one presence. I have known many betrothed young men, and I never yet knew one who paid the girl he loved so little courtesy as to flirt, ever so slightly, with another."

She could not see the flush that burned his face, for he knew that every word she uttered was but too true. He felt guilty in her sweet, innocent presence. Had he but loved her, he would have found no pleasure whatever in Iris Vincent's dangerous coquetries.

He would not have encouraged her by smile, word, or deed.

A wave of pity swept over his heart for Dorothy as he looked down into the pure, uplifted face. But it was only short-lived, for at that instant he heard Iris' silvery laughter from an adjoining room.

"I propose that we finish this interesting subject at some future time," he said, carelessly. "I have some important letters to write, and if you will excuse me for a little while, I should be very glad."

Sorrowfully Dorothy rose from the hassock and slowly quitted the room.

With lagging steps she made her way to her own room, her heart as heavy as lead in her bosom.

She had entered the library with buoyant steps and a light heart; aye, even a little snatch of song on her lips, for she had made up her mind that she would wait there until Harry came and have a good talk with him.

She had been so sure that he would take her in his arms and soothe away her fears, laughing at them in his own way as being the most ridiculous fancies which her sensitive little brain had conjured up.

And ah! how different had been the reality.

He had rudely repulsed her—and she his promised wife! Katy noticed how gloomy she was, and ran quickly to her young mistress' side.

"Oh, Miss Dorothy," she cried, "you do look so pale. Let me place you in a chair and bring you some wine."

Dorothy shook her head.

"I am not ill, Katy," she said, wearily, "only I—I have a slight headache. If you will leave me by myself I will take a short rest if I can, then I shall be all right."

But Katy insisted upon bringing her a cordial, if not the wine, and surely she was forgiven for putting a few drops of a sleeping potion in the glass ere she handed it to her mistress. She well knew that she had not slept soundly for some time past.

Surely she was breaking down slowly from some terrible mental strain. She realized but too well what that mental strain was.

Dorothy allowed her to lead her passively to the sofa, and to deposit her among the cushions.

"You will ring when you want me, Miss Dorothy," she said, placing a table with a bell on it close by her side.

"Yes," said Dorothy, wearily. "Now go and leave me, that's a good girl;" and Katy passed into the next apartment, drawing the curtains softly behind her. There she sat down and waited until her mistress should fall asleep. It almost made the girl's heart bleed to hear the great sighs that broke from Dorothy's lips.

"Poor soul! poor soul!" she cried; "how unhappy she is!"

But soon the potion began to take effect, and the sighs soon melted into deep, irregular breathing, and then Katy knew that she slept.

An hour passed, and yet another, still she did not waken, though there were loud sounds of mirth and revelry in the drawing-room beneath. The maid recognized Iris' voice and that of Harry Kendal.

"The grand rascal!" muttered the girl; "how I feel like choking that man! He doesn't care any more for that poor blind girl in there, that he's engaged to, than the dust which sticks to his patent leather shoes. I believe the truth is slowly beginning to dawn upon her."

At that moment she heard Dorothy's voice calling her, and she went quickly to her side.

"Oh, how long have I slept, Katy?" she cried.

"An hour or such a matter," responded the girl. "They have all been to dinner, but I thought sleep would be better for you."

"How long since?" cried Dorothy, springing from the sofa. "And did they not send up for me?" asking both questions in a breath, and waiting with feverish impatience for an answer.

"No," said the girl, bluntly.

"Did they forget me?" whispered Dorothy, in a voice so hollow that the tone frightened the little maid.

"It looks very much like it, Miss Dorothy," she answered; "but I did not forget you; I brought you up a whole trayful of things."

"I can not eat," sighed Dorothy, and she murmured under her breath: "Yes, they forgot me—forgot me! Come here, my good girl," she went on, very nervously; "there is something I want you to do for me."

Katy came close to her side. Dorothy reached out her hand and caught the girl's arm in her trembling grasp.

"I want you to slip down quietly, Katy," she said—"mind, very quietly—and see what they are doing down in the drawing-room. I hear Mr. Kendal's voice and Miss Vincent's. Take notice if Mrs. Kemp is with them, or if they are alone."

"Are you going down to-night, Miss Dorothy?" asked Katy.

"If it isn't too late," she answered, in a tremulous voice, adding: "I want you to lay out the prettiest dress I have, and some nice ribbon for my hair, before you go. I can be dressing while you are gone; it will save that much time."

Katy did as she was bid, and a few moments later was creeping noiselessly down the back stairway, which led to the drawing-room. Drawing the heavy silken *portières* aside, she peered cautiously in. As she expected, Mr. Kendal and Miss Vincent were enjoying each other's society, quite alone. But that was not the worst of it.

Chapter XVII.

Katy gazed long and earnestly at the picture before her.

Miss Vincent sat at the piano, magnificently dressed in a pale blue chiffon evening dress, with great clusters of pink roses at her belt, at her throat, and in the meshes of her jetty curls.

Beside her, turning over the music, and bending like a lover over her, was Harry Kendal.

And as the girl watched she saw him suddenly lift to his lips the little white hand that was straying over the keys.

"Do let me persuade you to sing for me, Iris," he was saying. "In what have I so far offended you that you are so ungracious to me this evening, Iris?" he murmured, reproachfully.

"I do not know that I am any different to-night from what I have always been," pouted the beauty. "I simply do not feel like singing, that is all."

"You have changed your mood very suddenly, Iris," he declared. "You asked me to come into the drawing-room to hear you sing, and now you tell me that you have changed your mind. What am I to think?"

"Whatever you please," she answered, curtly.

"Tell me one thing, Iris," he murmured, a little hoarsely, bending nearer over the pretty, willful coquette; "were the words of the song you intended to sing suggestive of a sudden coldness between two very near and very dear friends?"

"I will not listen to you!" cried Iris, petulantly.

"I repeat, what have I done to offend you, my dear girl?" he cried.

"Say to yourself that it was surely not my intention nor my will. You asked me to come to the library to listen to some poems. When I stepped into the room I saw at a glance that you had quite forgotten the appointment, Harry, by the picture that met my glance."

He knew in an instant to what she referred—he sitting in the arm-chair with Dorothy by his side, her arms twined about him.

"I did not ask her in there, Iris," he said, huskily. "I found her in there when I entered the apartment. She was evidently waiting for me. She met me with tears and reproaches, and if there is anything that is detestable to a man it is that line of conduct, believe me."

Iris shrugged her shoulders, but made no reply.

"Why did you not come in when you came to the door?" he asked, bending dangerously near the fatally beautiful face so near his own.

"Because I thought that two was company—three would be a crowd," she responded, proudly tossing back her jetty curls.

"*You* would always be welcome to *me*, Iris," he said, huskily. "You know that but too well by this time, don't you?" and his hand closed tightly over the one lying lightly in her lap, and his head drooped nearer still.

"Great Scott! they are almost kissing each other, the two vipers!" panted Katy to herself, her blood fairly boiling in her veins at the sight of this billing and cooing. "Oh, if I only dared put poor Miss Dorothy on her guard!"

She could not refrain from bursting in upon them at this critical instant, and in less time than it takes to tell it she had bounded into the room.

"A-hem, a-hem!" she coughed, pantingly; "but if you please, miss," turning and addressing herself to Iris, "the housekeeper is looking for you, and wants you to come to her."

"Certainly," said Iris, springing up from the piano stool with a face flushed as red as a peony and a very confused look in her eyes; "I will go at once;" and with an assumed smile on her face she glided from the room, muttering below her breath:

"I'd like to choke that little imp of a maid! Whenever I am talking to Harry Kendal, if I turn around I find her at my elbow."

Katy was about to follow Miss Vincent from the room, when Harry called to her.

"Remain a moment," he said. "I wish to see you."

With a little courtesy Katy obeyed.

For a moment or two he stood quite still in the center of the room, toying nervously with the medallion on his watch chain, and a very perceptible frown on his dark, handsome face.

"Tell me, how long have you been standing there, girl?"

She hung her head, but did not answer; but that silence told him quite as much as words.

"The wisest girls are those who never see or hear anything," he declared, eyeing her sharply.

Again Katy courtesied, making no reply. She knew quite well what he meant.

"I may as well come to the point and say that you are not to mention to any one anything that has taken place in this house—especially in this room to-night. Now here is something that may help you to remember the old adage that 'silence is golden.'" And as he spoke he thrust a bill into the girl's hand, motioning her from the drawing-room, and turning abruptly on his heel, he sauntered slowly across the room and flung himself down in an easy chair.

Katy hurried quickly upstairs.

"The grand rascal!" she muttered; "to pay me to help deceive Miss Dorothy! How my fingers tingled to box his ears! I longed to stamp my foot and cry out: 'You handsome villain—engaged to marry one young girl and making love to another! Oh! for shame! for shame!' It's a pity that Miss Dorothy hasn't a good big brother to give him the trouncing he so richly deserves. The Lord knows it's an unhappy life Miss Dorothy will lead with him, and it would be a blessing in disguise if something should happen to prevent the marriage from taking place. As for that sly, black minx, Iris Vincent, she must have a soul as hard as adamant and cruel as death to cheat a poor blind girl out of her lover, and to try all her arts to win him from her. They fairly make love to each other in her very presence; and she, poor soul! never knows it, because she is blind! The curse of God will surely fall on them, and they will be punished for their treachery to poor Miss Dorothy—and she so trustful and innocent! I wish I could think of some plan to break that up. Goodness knows, I wouldn't do such a thing for anything in the wide world. I have always believed that the angels take terrible vengeance upon any girl who takes another girl's lover from her by her wicked coquetries."

By this time she had reached Dorothy's *boudoir*. She found her young mistress waiting for her with the greatest impatience.

"Well," said Dorothy, quite as soon as she had opened the door, "who's down there?"

For an instant the inclination was strong within Katy's heart to tell the whole truth of what she had seen and heard. It was not the dollar, which seemed to burn in her pocket, that made her hold her tongue, but the fear of giving poor blind Dorothy pain, that caused her to hold her peace.

"Only Mr. Kendal, miss."

"I thought I heard voices," she said, wonderingly.

"Miss Vincent was there when I entered the room, but left a moment or so after," answered Katy, truthfully.

"Were they talking together? And what were they talking about?" asked Dorothy, eagerly.

"That I can not say, miss," returned the girl, flushing to the roots of her hair, and inwardly thankful that her poor young mistress could not see the distress which she knew must be mirrored on her face.

"Were they speaking so low that you could not hear them?" inquired Dorothy, quickly.

"Oh, no, miss! quite loud; but I was not listening."

Dorothy gave a sigh of relief.

"If it were not so late, I would go down stairs," she said, reflectively. "But then, there's the ball to-morrow night. I will be up late, so I suppose it would be just as well for me to rest to-night, for I want to look my best, Katy. I would give the world to look bright and gay as any girl there. I could hear the music, the patter of dancing feet, and the sound of merry laughter. And, oh, Katy! perhaps I might forget for a few brief moments my terrible affliction. I know Harry will be happy amid the brilliant throng, and that thought alone will be joy enough for me. You shall sit with me, Katy, to hold my wraps, my flowers, my fan, and—and you must watch sharp, and tell me, Katy, if he dances with any pretty girl the second time."

She felt that she must make a confidant of some one, even though it was Katy, the maid.

"You must not think for one moment I am jealous, Katy," she said, "for I assure you I am not; only as host I should not like him to pay too much courtesy to any one person, you know."

"Certainly not," assented Katy.

"I have asked Iris what she intends to wear, but for some reason she does not tell me, so I want you to notice particularly what she has on, and if she looks very pretty. But then, I think she is sure to look nice."

"I shall look very closely, you may be sure of that," responded Katy, "and tell you of everything that goes on—who's dancing, and who's sitting in corners flirting, and just who Mr. Kendal dances with. Will he take you in to supper, miss?" she asked, suddenly.

She was sorry the moment after that she had asked the question, for Dorothy's poor, sightless eyes filled with great tears.

"You know that he would like to," she murmured, faintly, "but it would be a ghastly sight—a poor blind girl sitting at the festal board with the gay guests. Oh! why did God put such a terrible affliction upon me?" throwing out her little white hands and beating the air as she sobbed aloud in her agony. "Why can I not enter into his joys, and share them with him as others do? Oh, Katy! will I not make but a sorry wife for my handsome king—my idol? I wonder what he can find about me to hold me still dear in his eyes, for I am no longer pretty, willful, madcap Dorothy, as they once called me."

Chapter XVIII.

The night of the ball came at last—the night which had been looked forward to so anxiously for weeks by many a maiden and brave swain.

By the time night had drawn her sable curtains over the sleeping earth all the preparations had been completed at Gray Gables, and when the lights were lighted it presented such a brilliant spectacle that those who witnessed never forgot it.

The guests began to arrive early, in order to have a long evening of enjoyment.

Late that afternoon an odd discussion had arisen which came near wrecking the whole affair.

Mrs. Kemp, Iris, and Dorothy were all seated in the general sitting-room discussing the last but by no means least important matter of who should receive the guests.

"You are the young lady of the house," said Mrs. Kemp, turning to Dorothy with a puzzled air, "and of course every one expects you to perform that pleasant duty; but—"

"Oh, no, no!" cut in Dorothy. "My—my affliction makes that an impossibility. *You* must do it, Mrs. Kemp."

"Really, child, my presence is so much of a necessity in looking after the servants and overlooking affairs in general that I assure you I can not be spared even for a brief half hour; so, as near as I can see, Iris must take your place for that occasion, with Mr. Kendal, to welcome your guests. What do you say, my dear?" she asked, turning anxiously to the beauty, who sat disconsolately by the window, listening to the conversation, feeling confident as to how the debate must end—in *her own* favor.

"I'm sure I do not mind doing so, if the arrangement suits Mr. Kendal and—Dorothy."

Harry entered the room at this stage, and of course the matter was quickly laid before him.

"Why, yes, Iris can help me receive the guests," he declared. "What a happy thought! I supposed I alone was to be delegated to that task. Yes, let us settle it in that manner, by all means."

As usual, no one thought of consulting Dorothy's opinion. Indeed, they scarcely missed her presence when, a few moments later, she slipped from the room to have a good cry over the matter.

Katy was startled as she beheld her white face as she groped her way into the room. She sat so still that Dorothy imagined herself quite alone.

"I—I can not bear it!" she sobbed, flinging herself face downward on the carpet with a wretched little sob. "In everything she seems to come between me and my lover! Oh, I wish to Heaven that Iris Vincent would go away! Harry has not been the same to me since she has been beneath this roof. They tell me it is my imagination, but my heart tells me it is no idle fancy. *She* will be standing by my lover's side receiving *my* guests! Oh, angels up in Heaven, forgive me if the pangs of jealousy, cruel as death, spring up in my poor heart at that bitter thought!" And another thought: "Harry is beginning to depend so much upon her society. Now, if I ask, 'Where is Harry?' the answer is, 'Out driving or walking or singing with Iris.' Katy tells me she is very plain of face—nay, even homely. If she were beautiful I should be in terror too horrible for words. It is wicked of me, but, oh! I can not help but thank God she is not fair of face, to attract my darling from me."

Tears rolled down Katy's cheeks as she listened. Not for the world would she have let her poor young mistress know that her grief had had a witness. She kept perfectly quiet, making no sound, scarcely breathing, until Dorothy passed slowly into an inner apartment, and she was heartily glad that she touched her bell a moment after.

Katy hurried to her with alacrity, taking pains, however, to tiptoe to the door, open it, and close it again, quite as if she had just come in from the corridor.

"Now, Katy," said her young mistress, "you must make haste to help me dress. I am impatient. I feel dreadfully nervous, as though a great calamity was to take place. I feel just such a strange sensation as seemed to clutch at my heart before that terrible accident happened that has blighted my whole life."

"Oh, dear Miss Dorothy, *please* don't talk so!" cried Katy, aghast. "I'm sure it isn't right, if I may make so bold as to say so to you. I have always heard it said: 'Never cross a bridge of trouble until you come to it.'"

"'Coming events cast their shadows before,'" quoted Dorothy, slowly.

"I have made your dress look so lovely, Miss Dorothy," she cried, bravely attempting to turn her thoughts into another channel, "and it's right sorry I am that you can't see it. Every one will say that it is the prettiest dress at the ball. You said I might fix it any way that I liked, so long as it looked grand."

"How have you arranged it, Katy?" asked Dorothy, with a faint smile, being girl enough to forget her sorrow for an instant in speaking of her ball dress.

"It is your new white tulle, miss, that I picked out—the one that you had made to go to parties in, providing you were ever asked to any, the first week you came to Gray Gables, you remember."

"Oh, yes," murmured Dorothy, clasping her little hands. "I—I remember so well how nice it looked on me, too."

"You looked like an angel in it!" declared Katy; resuming: "Well, it's that one, miss, and I have been embroidering flowers all over the front of it as a surprise for you, and, oh, they look perfectly magnificent on it!—just as though some one stood near you and threw a great handful of blossoms over you and they clung to your white tulle dress just where they fell."

"What kind of flowers are they?" asked Dorothy, delightedly.

"Wisteria blossoms," said Katy.

Dorothy sprang to her feet, pale as death.

"You have embroidered purple wisteria blossoms all over my ball dress?" she whispered, in an awful voice.

"Yes," returned the girl, wondering what was coming next.

"Oh, Katy!" she cried, in a choking voice, "don't you know that purple wisteria blossoms mean tears?"

"I don't believe in all those old women's superstitions, miss," declared Katy, stoutly. "I imagine that it was got up by some muddy-complexioned creature, whose only annoyance was that the pretty blossoms didn't look good on her, and consequently she gave them a bad name to keep others from wearing them. There's plenty of such things being done."

This explanation, or rather explosion of the pet superstition, amused Dorothy vastly.

"Well, I shall not mind the old adage about wisteria blossoms and tears. I'll wear the dress anyhow, Katy, come what may. But do you know what Iris is going to wear? I haven't been able to find out."

"Nor has any one, ma'am," muttered Katy. "She has been making up her ball dress in her own room for the past fortnight, and keeps the door securely fastened; but we shall see very soon now, for it is quite time to dress, and she has to be ready first to receive the guests. I heard Mr. Kendal telling her so, a few moments since, as they passed through the corridor just as I opened the door."

She saw Dorothy turn a shade paler, and her head drooped, but she made no reply.

"Shall I commence now to arrange your toilet?" she asked, anxious to dress her mistress, and then don her own new dress for the gala occasion.

"I don't want to go into the ball-room until all the guests have arrived, and then I want to slip in quietly," said Dorothy; "so you need not hurry."

It was a sorry task at best for Katy, dressing her poor, blind mistress for the ball.

Ah! it was pitiful to see her sitting so patiently there with her back to the mirror, while the maid, with great tears rolling down her cheeks, fastened the clouds of tulle here and there with the dark blossoms, and twined them in the golden curls that fell about her white neck.

Oh, how radiantly fair she looked! And Katy knew that no one gazing in those beautiful violet eyes would ever realize that the lovely girl was blind—stone blind.

Her hand trembled violently as, an hour later, she clung to her maid's arm, and timidly, shrinkingly entered the great ball-room crowded with guests. No one noticed their entrance, the throng was so great, and she had her heart's desire. She slipped into a corner without her presence being commented on.

She did not know that a little place among a bower of ferns had been previously arranged for her by Katy, where she could sit and hear the music without being seen herself; nor would Katy be seen by the guests.

"Tell me," she whispered, nervously clutching the girl's hand, "where is Harry, and is—is Miss Vincent with him, and how does she look?"

Before Katy could frame a reply the last question was rudely answered by a stranger. Two young ladies at that instant dropped down into seats so near Dorothy that she could easily have touched them had she reached out her hand from her screen of palms and roses.

"What a magnificent-looking girl that Iris Vincent is!" cried one of the young girls. "The fame of her great beauty is spreading everywhere; but I never dreamed she was as beautiful as the description I have heard of her, and I find she far surpasses it. I wonder that poor, blind Dorothy Glenn is not jealous that her affianced husband should pay the girl so much attention."

"This is the first time I have seen her," replied her companion, "and I, too, am amazed at her marvelous beauty. As I stepped into the ball-room she was the first person I beheld, and she has dazzled my eyes ever since. Oh, it was a wonderful picture she made, standing under a slender palm tree, in her white tulle dress flecked with gold and pearls, and those blood-red rubies encircling her white throat and perfect arms and coiled in her jetty curls; and then those glorious dark eyes! No wonder men lose their hearts over her at the first fatal glance into their wonderful, mesmeric depths. She is fairer than the fairest of poets' dreams."

Dorothy listened with bated breath, then turned quickly to Katy.

"Have you deceived me—*me*, a poor blind girl?" she cried in a terrible voice that sounded like a cry from the tomb. "You told me that the girl who had come beneath this roof was homely and terribly plain. *They* say she is beautiful. Oh, God! have you deceived me? I must know the truth at once."

Chapter XIX.

"Katy," repeated Dorothy, in a shrill, awful whisper, "tell me, have you willfuly deceived me? You have said Miss Vincent was plain—nay, more, that she was homely—and on all sides of me I hear them speaking of her wonderful beauty."

Katy sank back shivering in her seat.

"It's fine feathers that make fine birds to-night," she rejoined, faintly. "No wonder they think Iris Vincent looks well to-night. She's rigged out like a real peacock; and her face is painted, too. I can see it clear across the room; and I am quite sure that Mr. Kendal has noticed it; and I've heard him say that if there's anything which he detests, it's girls who whiten their faces with chalk."

Still Dorothy did not feel comforted. A nameless fear which she could scarcely define by words had crept into her heart, and a smoldering flame of jealousy burst suddenly forth; and that was the beginning of a terrible end.

She leaned wearily back in her seat, and looked so white that Katy was frightened.

"Shall I get you a glass of ice-water, Miss Dorothy?" she cried.

The pale lips murmured assent, and she flew to do her mistress' bidding.

Left to herself, Dorothy sprang hastily to her feet.

"It almost seems as if I shall go mad!" she murmured—"yes, mad—with this terrible fear clutching at my heart! I must have air. I am stifling!"

All unmindful of the errand upon which she had sent Katy, Dorothy rose hastily to her feet, and, remembering that there was a rear entrance leading from the ball-room near where she sat, she groped her way thither.

The night air fanned her feverish cheek, but it did not cool the fever in her brain or the fire that seemed eating into her very heart. A thousand fancies, so weird and strange that they terrified her, seemed to take possession of her brain. She had relied so entirely upon what they had told her—that Miss Vincent was very plain—that the feeling of jealousy had never before occurred to her; for well she knew that Harry Kendal was a beauty-worshiper, and that no matter how much he might be thrown in contact with a girl who was plain of face, he would never dream of being anything else than simply courteous to her.

Now affairs seemed to take on a new and hideous form.

She recalled each and every incident that had taken place since Miss Vincent's arrival, and

"Trifles light as airSeemed confirmation strong as Holy Writ"

as she viewed them now.

"Even the guests notice how attentive he is to her," she said to herself, with a bitter sob, wringing her cold little hands and clutching them tightly over her heart.

Suddenly she heard the sound of voices, and sank down upon a seat at hand until they should pass by.

She did not know that the seat which she had selected on the broad piazza was directly back of one of the large, vine-wreathed, fluted pillars, and in the dense shadow.

This time she readily divined that the voices must belong to two light-hearted, happy girls.

"Are you having a good time, Grace, dear?" asked one.

"Oh, quite the jolliest I have ever had in all my life!" was the reply. "I haven't missed one dance, and all my partners have been so handsome—quite the prettiest fellows in the ball-room! And how is it with you?"

"Oh, I'm enjoying myself, too!" laughed the other girl, "But did you notice what a ninny I had in that last waltz-quadrille? Don't you hate partners who stand away off, and barely touch your finger-tips as they dance with you? Upon my word, I'd rather have the straight-as-a-mackerel kind, who hold you so tight you can scarcely catch your breath!"

And at this both girls went off into uproarious laughter, when suddenly one of them exclaimed:

"Have you yet had a waltz with handsome Harry Kendal?"

"No," returned the other, ruefully. "At the last ball I went to he was almost wild to put his name down for every waltz with me. But, after all, I can not wonder at that when I see how greatly he is infatuated with the beauty of the ball to-night—the fair Iris Vincent."

"Have you heard all the talk to-night about that?" chimed in the other, her voice sinking to a low, confidential tone. "Every one has noticed it, and it is the talk of the ball-room."

"It is shameful for him to carry on so," returned her companion, "when every one knows that his wedding day with poor, blind Dorothy Glenn is so near at hand."

"Do you know," said the other, slowly, "that I doubt if he will ever marry Dorothy now? You must remember that he became engaged to her before that terrible accident. And do you know there is great diversity of opinion as to whether the poor fellow should marry her or not. It is very nice to read about in books—of lovers proving true to their *fiancées* through every trouble and tribulation—but I tell you they don't do it in real life. When trouble comes to a girl, nine lovers out of ten fly from her 'to seek pastures new;' and, after all, to come right down to the fine point, between you and me, could you really blame Harry Kendal if he were to break off with Dorothy? He is young and handsome, and I say that it would be a bitter shame for him to go through life with a blind girl for a wife; and when I think of it I actually feel indignant with the girl for holding him to his engagement under such circumstances. She ought to know that in time he would actually hate her for it. She can share none of his joys. Why, she would be only a pitiful burden to handsome Harry Kendal! That girl whom he seems so infatuated with would be a thousand times more suitable for him. Oh, what a handsome couple they do make! And every one can see, though they think they hide it so well, how desperately they are in love with each other."

They moved on, little dreaming of the ruin and blight they had left behind them.

They were scarcely out of hearing when the great cry that had been choked back so long burst forth in a wild, piercing wail of agony that meant the breaking then and there of a human heart. But the dance-music inside, to which the joyous, merry feet kept time, completely drowned it.

Dorothy had risen from her chair, and the look on her face was terrible to behold.

"Let me quite understand it," she whispered—"let me try to realize and grasp the awful truth: Harry Kendal, my lover, has ceased to care for me, and is lavishing his attention, nay, more, his affection, upon another and one who in return loves him; and they say that I should give him up to her—I, who love him better than my own life! He is all I have left me in my terrible affliction, and they would take even him from me and give him to another. They said it was not right for me to cling to him, and to burden him with a blind wife through life—that the thought is torture to him. Oh, God in Heaven! can it be true?"

And again the angels at the great White Throne were startled with the piercing cries of woe that broke from the girl's white lips, which once more the dance-music mercifully drowned.

"I will go to him and confront him with what I have heard. He shall choose between us before all the people assembled here to-night. I will fling myself upon my knees at his feet, crying out: 'Oh, my darling! my love! my life! tell me that the cruel rumors which I have heard are false—that you do not hate me because—because of the awful affliction that Heaven has seen fit to put upon me! Turn from the girl by your side to me—to me, your promised bride! She can never love you as I do. You are my all—my world! If I were to die to-day—aye, within this hour—my soul could not leave this earth while you were here! I would cling to you in life or in death!'"

With a swift motion Dorothy turned and re-entered the house, forgetful of her blindness, and to count the steps which she had taken, remembering only that she was undergoing the greatest trial of her life.

Swift as a fluttering swallow she hastened across the broad piazza, but in the confusion of her whirling brain she had mistaken the direction.

One instant more, too quick for a cry, too quick for a moan, she had stepped off the veranda, and fell with a terrible thud down five feet below, and lay, stunned and unconscious, on the graveled walk.

The shock was so sudden, so terrible that surely God in His mercy was kind in that the fearful pain of the fall was not realized by her.

The moments dragged themselves wearily by as she lay there. Fully half an hour elapsed. No one missed her save Katy, no one thought of looking for her out in the cold and darkness, which was penetrated only by the dim light of the stars. The dew of night fell silently, pityingly upon the white, upturned face and curling golden hair, which lay tangled among the sharp pebbles. Gradually consciousness dawned upon her brain. The warm blood crept back to the chilled veins and pulsed feebly, but with it came the remembrance of the terrible blow that had fallen upon her.

Dorothy staggered to her feet, but as she did so a strange electric shock seemed to pass through her body and balls of fire to whirl before her eyes. But as they cleared away a great cry broke from the girl's lips:

"Oh, God! can it be true? Heaven has restored my sight to me as miraculously as it was taken from me!"

Once again she saw the blue sky, with its myriads of golden-hearted stars, bending over her; the great stone house, with its lighted windows, and beyond, the tall, dark oak trees, with their great, widespread tossing branches; and she fell upon her knees and kissed the very stones at her feet and the green blades of waving grass that she never once thought she would see again, and she raised her white arms to heaven with such piteous cries of thankfulness that the angels must have heard and wept over.

Yes, Dorothy's sight had been restored to her as miraculously as it had been taken from her.

But even in the midst of her great joy the dregs of woe still lingered as memory brought back to her the terrible ordeal through which she had passed.

With bated breath she turned and crept swiftly back to the house and up to the long windows that opened out on the porch, sobbing bitterly to herself that she would see at last if her lover was true or false to her.

Chapter XX.

With her heart throbbing with the most intense excitement, Dorothy pushed aside the great clusters of crimson creepers and thick green leaves, pressed her white face close against the window-pane, and gazed in upon the gorgeous scene.

For an instant the great blaze of light dazzled her weak eyes, and everything seemed to swim before her.

But gradually, little by little, she began to distinguish objects, and at last her eyes fell upon the face of Harry Kendal.

With a great cry, the girl clutched her hands tightly over her heart. She never thought that she would look upon his face again in this world.

It was *his* face—the face of her hero, her king, before which all else paled as the moonbeams pale before the glaring light of the rising sun. Then suddenly she saw the face beside him into which he was gazing, and it was then that the heart in her bosom almost turned to stone.

Never in all her life had she beheld such a vision of loveliness, and she knew in an instant that the proud beauty must be Iris Vincent.

Slowly Dorothy crept around to the other side of the porch, up to the window, that she might have a better view of them, and perhaps she could hear what they were saying.

But as she reached it, to her great disappointment she saw them link arms and stroll out of the ball-room toward the conservatory, and thither she bent her steps, intent upon reaching it before they did.

She had barely screened herself behind a tall *jardinière* of roses and flowering plants, ere, laughing and chattering, the two entered the floral bower.

"The ball is a grand success, Iris," he was saying, gayly; "they all seem to be enjoying themselves immensely. How is it with you?"

"It is a night that will stand out forever in my life," she responded, glancing up at him with those dangerously dark eyes, and a smile on her red lips.

The girl who watched them breathlessly from behind the roses clutched her hands over her heart.

The sight maddened her. They were so near each other, their heads bent so close; and while she gazed, suddenly Kendal bent still closer and kissed the girl's lips.

Dorothy tried to cry aloud, to spring out and confront them. Her brain reeled; the blood, chill as ice, stood still in her veins, and without a cry, or even a moan she sank down unconscious in her hiding-place.

"What is that sound?" cried Iris, with a start.

"Only some of the clumsy servants in the corridor without," replied Kendal. "But, Iris, are you trying to avoid me? I have brought you here to tell you something, and you must listen. The time has come when we must fully understand each other. You know quite as well as I that the life we are leading, Iris, can not go on like this forever. From the first moment we met the attraction I felt toward you changed the whole current of my life."

Iris hid her face in the bouquet of white hyacinths which she carried.

"It is too late to talk of that now," she murmured. "Your heart went out to another before—before I met you."

"There is such a thing as affections waning when one discovers that one's heart is not truly mated, Iris," he cried.

She did not answer; and thus emboldened by her silence, he went on, huskily:

"Let me give you the whole history of my meeting with Dorothy Glenn, from first to last, and you will understand the situation better. You can realize, Iris, that an acquaintance which commences through a flirtation, as it were, can never end in true love. Such an acquaintance is not a lasting one. Come and sit down on this rustic seat, Iris, and listen; and as we sit here in the dim, mellow light, you shall judge me, and your decision shall seal my fate."

At the self-same moment in which Harry Kendal was beginning his narrative, there was quite a commotion at the outer gate which guarded the main entrance of Gray Gables.

One of the servants, lounging lazily at his post of duty, was suddenly startled out of the doze into which he had fallen by the shadow of a woman flitting hurriedly past him.

"Hold on, there! Hold on, I say! Who are you, and what do you want?"

A figure clad in a long dark cloak, hooded and veiled, stopped short with a little exclamation, which he could not quite catch.

"Hold on, there! Where are you going?" he repeated, springing to her side. "There is something going on here to-night. You can't enter these grounds until I know who you are and what your business is."

"This is Gray Gables, is it not?" exclaimed a tremulous voice from behind the veil.

"I should have supposed you would have found that out before you entered the grounds," declared the man, suspiciously.

She saw her mistake, and started.

"I only wanted to make sure that I was right," she said, apologetically. "I—I have business with the housekeeper; I want to see her."

Before she could utter another word he whistled sharply. His call brought a small lad to his side.

"Tell Mrs. Kemp there's a young woman here who would like to see her. What name, please?" he asked, abruptly, turning to the veiled figure.

"I—I am afraid she wouldn't know; but you might, mention the name— Miss Mead"—this rather stutteringly.

Very soon the answer came back that the housekeeper did not know Miss Mead, and hadn't time to see strangers.

"But I must see her!" implored the excited voice from behind the thick veil. "Do let me go to the house to her. I will detain her but a moment, I assure you. She would be so sorry if she missed seeing me."

With no suspicion of the terrible catastrophe that was to follow on the heels of it, the man without further ado allowed her to pass.

The stranger sped quickly up the graveled walk, and, as Dorothy had done but a short time before, drew cautiously up to the brilliantly lighted window, threw back her veil, and peered breathlessly in upon the gorgeous scene.

As the light fell athwart her, you and I, dear reader, can easily recognize the marble-white face of—Nadine Holt.

"So!" she muttered, between her clinched teeth, "I have tracked my false, perfidious lover to his home at last. When Harry Kendal lighted the fire of love in my heart, he little knew that the blaze would in time consume himself. I am not one to be made love to and cast off at will, as he shall soon see.

"From the hour that he eloped with Dorothy Glenn, on that memorable Labor Day, life lost all its charms for me, and I vowed to Heaven that I would find them, and deal out vengeance to them. They crushed my heart, and now I shall crush theirs. Ah, how I watched for him in the crowded streets, the ferries, and on the elevated roads!

"I believed sooner or later that I should find him, and I was right. Only a week ago I met him face to face, but he did not know me because of the thick veil I wore. I might have raised my veil and he would never have recognized in the pinched and haggard features the countenance of Nadine Holt, whose beauty he was wont to praise so lavishly. Ah, the traitor!

"He turned into a florist's shop, and he never dreamed who the woman was who entered the place and stood silently beside him while he gave the order for the great decorations for the grand ball which was to take place at his home in Gray Gables, in Yonkers, a fortnight from that date.

"When he quitted the shop I flew out after him; but all in an instant he disappeared from my sight as though the ground had suddenly opened and swallowed him. But I laughed aloud. What cared I then. I knew just where to find him. The place was written indelibly on my brain in letters of fire—Gray Gables, Yonkers!

"Only Heaven knows how I have worked to get a day off and to earn extra money to make this little trip! And now I am here to face him. Is he married to Dorothy Glenn, I wonder? It would take only that knowledge to make a fiend incarnate of me!"

At that moment one of the servants passing along the porch stopped short at sight of the young woman in black, with the death-white face and flashing black eyes, peering into the ball-room from the long porch window.

"They are having a great time in there," he said, jerking his head with a nod in the direction of the ball-room.

"Yes!" returned Nadine Holt, sharply.

Then it occurred to her that she could find out something about the lover who had deserted her. And there was another thing which puzzled her greatly. The name which he had given the florist was not the one by which she had known him—she would find out all by this man. Now he was calling himself Mr. Harry Kendal—that was the name he had given the florist.

"In whose honor is the ball given, my good fellow?" she asked, with an assumption of carelessness.

For a moment he looked stupidly at her.

"I mean, who is giving the ball?" she added.

"Oh, it's Mr. Kendal, ma'am—leastwise, he and Miss Dorothy are giving it together."

She started as though a serpent had stung her, then stood perfectly still and looked at the man with gleaming eyes.

"Miss Dorothy—who?" she asked, knowing full well what his answer must be.

"Miss Dorothy Glenn, ma'am," he replied. "But she won't be 'miss' very long, for she is soon to marry Mr. Kendal."

"Soon to marry him!" she repeated, vaguely, saying in the next breath, "then they are not *already* married," muttering the words more to herself than to the man. "Where does this girl, Dorothy live?" she asked, suddenly.

"That I couldn't say, ma'am," he replied. "I only came to Gray Gables to-day, to work. I know only the little that I have heard the servants say while at their work this afternoon. They say Miss Dorothy is very beautiful."

Chapter XXI.

The white face into which the man gazed grew whiter still, the eyes dilated, and her heart twinged with a pang of jealousy more bitter than death to endure.

People always made that remark when speaking of Dorothy. It was that fatal gift which had won her lover from her, Nadine said to herself, and which had wrecked her life.

Oh! if she could but destroy that pink-and-white beauty!

The thought was born in Nadine Holt's breast all in an instant, and seemed to fire her whole being.

She knew her lover's passionate adoration of a beautiful face, and then and there the thought came to her: How long would he love Dorothy Glenn if that pretty pink-and-white face were seamed and scarred?

She laughed—a low, strange, eerie laugh that quite startled the man as he walked away.

Left to herself, Nadine Holt deliberately opened the hall door and stole into the house. She had but one purpose in view, and that was to confront her lover and Dorothy before all the invited guests.

There was nothing about the dark figure to attract especial attention, and she glided through the corridor unnoticed.

Was it the hand of fate most terrible that guided her toward the conservatory? The dark figure glided like a shadow toward the open door, and then paused abruptly, for the low sound of voices fell upon her ear, and one of them she recognized as that of her perfidious lover.

Through the softened pearly gloom she saw him sitting on the rustic bench close—very close—to the slender, girlish figure in fleecy white, and the sight made the blood in her veins turn to molten fire.

Like an evil spirit she crept toward them. She would—she *must*—know what he was saying to his companion in that leafy bower.

She said to herself, of course it was Dorothy, and that they had stolen away from the lights and the music for a few tender words with each other, after the fashion of love-sick lovers.

It had not been so very long ago since he had been talking with her in just that lover-like way, only their courtship had taken place in the public parks, sitting on the benches, or walking lovingly arm in arm along the crowded thoroughfares; and he had brought Dorothy to his own grand home—Dorothy, her hated rival!—to enjoy this paradise of a place, and to make love to her in this Eden bower of roses and scented, murmuring, tinkling fountains.

"Dorothy!" he murmured in his rich, low, musical voice. How plainly she heard the name! The rest of the sentence she could not catch, though she crept nearer and nearer, and strained every nerve to listen. "I love you as I have never loved anything in this life before," she heard him say, "and my future without you would be unendurable. I can not endure it—I will not!"

The poor wretch who listened grew mad as she heard the tender words whispered into the ears of another by her false lover.

She crouched still lower, and her hand, as she threw it out wildly, came in contact with something hard and cold. It was a long, thin, sharp-bladed knife which the gardener had been using only that day to trim the bushes, and which, in his hurry, he had carelessly forgotten. She realized instantly what it was, and, with the thought, a diabolical idea crept into her brain.

"Why should Dorothy Glenn live to enjoy the smiles of the man whose love she has robbed me of," she muttered below her breath, "while my heart hungers and my soul quivers in endless torture for the affection that is denied me? I can endure it no longer!"

The mad desire to spoil the fair beauty of her rival overpowered her until the thought possessed her and rendered her almost a fiend incarnate.

Grasping the long, sharp-bladed knife tightly, Nadine Holt raised her right arm slowly, cautiously. Not so much as a leaf rustled to warn the two sitting on the rustic bench of the terrible danger that hung over them.

Harry Kendal's low, musical voice sank to a lower cadence. He drew the slender figure of the girl nearer and that action was fatal.

There was a quick, whizzing sound, followed by an awful cry of terror from Iris, and Kendal's hand, resting lightly about her waist, was deluged in blood.

"Murder! murder! Oh, heavens!" shrieked Iris, and she fell at his feet in a swoon.

In the commotion Nadine Holt turned like a pantheress and made her escape from the conservatory and from the house.

"Murder! murder!" Those terrible cries that rent the air were the first sounds that Dorothy heard as her benumbed brain gained consciousness. And as she staggered, benumbed and dazed, to her feet she almost fell over a slimy knife lying there, and at that instant a strong hand flung back the rose-vines and Harry Kendal, white and quivering with wrath, confronted her.

"Dorothy Glenn!" he cried, in a horrible voice fairly reverberating with intense emotion, "You! Oh, you cruel, wicked girl! You—you fiend! to do what you have done!" and reaching out his hand he flung her backward from him as though she were a scorpion whose very touch was contamination. "Fly up to your own room," he cried, hoarsely, "and do not leave it for a moment until I come to you there! Have nothing to say; refuse to speak to any one!" and catching her fiercely by the shoulder, he fairly dragged her through the conservatory toward the rear door, which communicated with a back stairway that led up to her room.

Faint and dazed, Dorothy had not offered the least resistance to this cruel treatment. Her brain seemed stupefied by the whirling, confusing events taking place so rapidly around her. She only realized two things: that she had betrayed her presence in the conservatory when she fell to the floor upon hearing her lover speak words of affection to her rival, and that Harry was bitterly angry with her for being there. She did not remember that she had lost consciousness. It seemed to her that as her senses were about leaving her strange cries recalled them.

It occurred to her that in his excitement and anger her lover had not noticed that she had regained her sight.

Wearily Dorothy ascended the steep, narrow stairway and entered her own room. A soft, low, dim light flooded the apartment, upon which she had not gazed for many and many a long day.

Katy was not there, and she flung herself into the nearest arm-chair, sobbing wretchedly, although on that night she had cause to cry out to Heaven and rejoice for God's mercy to her for so unexpectedly restoring her sight. But, ah, me! how strange it is that all the blessings Heaven can shower upon us seem as dross when the one love we crave proves fickle.

Dorothy did not have the heart to cry out joyfully and thankfully. Her head drooped on her breast with a low, quivering sigh, and her hands fell in her lap.

Suddenly something around the bottom of her dress caught her eye, and she started to her feet with a low cry.

"It is blood!" she cried out in an awful voice.

No sooner had the door closed behind Dorothy ere Kendal flew back to Iris' side.

No one had heard the terrible cries. He thanked Heaven for that. The music had drowned them.

He had quite believed that Iris was dying. A hasty examination showed him that it was only a slight wound on the shoulder, from which blood was flowing profusely.

"Thank God it is no worse!" he cried, breathing freely.

He quickly set about restoring Iris, and in a moment she opened her eyes.

"Murder! murder!" she would have cried again, but he put his hand instantly over her red lips.

"Hush! hush! in Heaven's name!" he cried. "You will alarm the whole household. You are not seriously hurt!"

"Some one was trying to murder me!" shrieked Iris, hysterically.

"No, no!" he returned, quickly. "Listen, Iris, for Heaven's sake! One of the panes of glass of the conservatory directly overhead was broken, and—and a little part of it fell in, grazing your shoulder. It is a deep and painful scratch, I can well understand; but it is only a scratch, I can assure you."

"Oh, it has ruined my dress!" cried the girl, in anger and dismay, never thinking for an instant of doubting the truth of his assertion. "I can not appear in the ball-room again. No one must know that we were here together," she went on, hastily—"not one human soul! You must give out that I—I became suddenly indisposed and went to my own room."

"Yes, I think your suggestions are best," he agreed.

The guests received this explanation of the sudden absence of the beauty of the ball with regret, and more than one whisper went the rounds of the room how this seemed to disturb handsome Harry Kendal, for his face was very pale, and he seemed so nervous.

At the earliest opportunity Harry Kendal slipped away from the merry throng and up to Dorothy's apartment, hastily knocking at the door.

She opened it herself.

"Step out into the corridor," he said, sternly; "I want to speak to you."

And trembling with apprehension caused by his stern manner, Dorothy obeyed.

She could see, even in the dim light, that his face was white as death.

"I have come to have an understanding with you, Dorothy Glenn!" he cried hoarsely. "Your dastardly action of to-night has forever placed a barrier between you and me! I am here to say this to you: here and now I sever our betrothal! The same roof shall no longer shelter us both! Either you leave this house to-night, or I'll go!"

Chapter XXII.

It was the most pitiful scene that pen could describe. The beautiful young girl, in her dress of fleecy white, with the faded purple blossoms on her breast entwined among the meshes of her disheveled golden hair, crouching back among the green leaves, and the white-faced, handsome, angry man clutching her white arm, crying out hoarsely that never again should they both breathe the same air beneath that roof—that she must leave Gray Gables within the hour, or he would.

"I did not know that I had done so terribly wrong," moaned the girl, shrinking back from those angry, fiery eyes that glowered down so fiercely into her own.

A laugh that was more horrible than the wildest imprecation could have been broke from his lips.

"You seem to have a remarkably mixed idea of right and wrong," he retorted, sternly, relaxing his hold and standing before her with rigid, folded arms, his anger growing more intense with each passing instant as he looked down into the girl's agonized face.

Had she done so very, very wrong in remaining in the conservatory, and in listening to her betrothed make love to her rival? she wondered vaguely.

Surely, she should have been the one to have cried out in bitter anger, not he.

"Let me tell you how it all came about," she gasped, faintly.

"I—I was in the ball-room with Katy, when it grew so warm that I sent for an ice. She did not return as soon as I had expected her, and—and I groped my way out into the garden to await her there. But as I stepped from the porch a wonderful thing happened, Harry. I—I missed my footing and fell headlong down the steps to the graveled walk below, and the shock restored my sight. Oh! look at me, Harry!" she exclaimed, with quivering intensity, holding out her white arms toward him. "I can see now. I can see your idolized face, oh, my beloved! I—I came here to tell you this—to tell you the wonderful tidings! I intended to send to the ball-room for you, but before I could put my intention into execution I—I heard steps approaching, and drew back among the screening leaves till they should pass. You came in with Iris Vincent, and I heard what you said, and my brain whirled—I grew dazed. You—you know the rest!"

He was not overwhelmed by the great tidings that she had regained her sight, as she had expected he would be. Instead, he retorted brusquely:

"It was a pity that your sight returned to you to enable you to do so dastardly a deed; and I am beginning to have my doubts whether or not you have not been duping us all along, and, under that guise, spying upon us—which seems to be your forte. This revelation makes me angrier than ever," he went on, "for it leaves you with no possible hope of pardon for your atrocious conduct, which merits the whole world's scorn and contempt!"

"I see it all!" cried Dorothy, springing to her feet and facing him. "You have prearranged this quarrel with me to break our betrothal, that you might wed your new love—Iris Vincent. But, just for pure spite, I will not release you—never! I will tell the whole world of your duplicity. An engagement is a solemn thing. It takes two to enter into it and two to break it."

The scorn on his handsome face deepened.

"I do not very well see how you can marry a man when he makes up his mind not to have you," he declared. "That is a difficult feat, and I shall have to see it done before I can be convinced that it can be accomplished," he replied, icily, adding: "There are many women in this world who would stand back and watch such a proceeding with the wildest anxiety, I imagine;" this sneeringly.

"You shall never marry Iris Vincent!" Dorothy panted. "I—I would prevent it at any cost. Once before you forsook me when I needed you most; you left me to die when I fell from the steamer down into the dark water, when we were returning from Staten Island, that never-to-be-forgotten night; so why should I be surprised at your willingness to desert me now?"

He turned on his heel.

"It is now two o'clock in the morning," he said. "My duty requires me to go down to the ball-room and bid the guests adieu as they take their departure, and when that is over I shall leave this house until this difficulty has been settled. The reading of Doctor Bryan's will is to take place at noon. I shall be present then, and after that—well—well, we shall see what will take place."

With these words Kendal quitted the room, and left Dorothy standing there with the tears falling like rain down her cheeks—surely the most piteous object in the whole wide world.

When Kendal found himself alone his intense anger against Dorothy began to cool a little.

"It is true she attempted to do a horrible deed," he muttered; "but I must not forget that love for me prompted her to it, and show her *some* mercy."

After all the guests had taken their departure, and the house had settled down into the darkness and quiet of the waning night, Kendal paced his room in a greatly perturbed state of mind, thinking the matter over.

He was terribly in love with Iris, he admitted to himself; but he had done wrong, fearfully wrong, in breaking off his engagement with Dorothy until after the reading of the will. Iris was beautiful, bewitching—his idea of all that a proud, imperious, willful sweetheart should be—but Dorothy would have what was much better than all this, the golden shekels; and then, too, now that the girl was no longer blind, she would have plenty of admirers; and he could have cursed himself for those hasty words, that no longer should she live under the same roof with himself.

It was daylight when he threw himself down on the bed, fairly worn out; and his head no sooner touched the pillow than he fell into a deep sleep, and it was almost noon ere he opened his eyes again, and then it was the slow, measured chime of the clock as it struck the half hour which awakened him.

"Great Heaven! half past eleven!" he ejaculated, springing from the couch. "I shall barely have time to get downstairs to be present at the reading of the will. I must make all haste; but first of all I must find out how Iris is, and if her shoulder pains her much."

He rang the bell hastily, and to the servant who answered the summons he gave his verbal message to Miss Vincent. But in a very short time the man returned, placing a letter in his hand.

Kendal was mystified, for he saw that it was Iris' delicate chirography. He tore open the envelope with the fever of impatience, and as his eye fell upon the delicately written lines his handsome face turned white as marble.

"My DEAR HARRY," it commenced, "you will feel greatly surprised at the contents of this letter. I think it best to break into the subject at once, and to tell you the plain truth of just what has happened.

"Shortly after I left you and retired to my own apartments the pain in my shoulder became so intense that, remembering there was a young surgeon among the invited guests, I sent for him at once. I can never tell you just exactly how it came about, but the upshot of the whole matter was that he asked me to marry him.

"I wanted time to consider it; but he said it must be then and there, within the hour, or never. I demurred, but he was resolute.

"I realized that I held my future in my own hands, and that I had to decide upon my own destiny at once.

"He is a millionaire's son, and you are only a poor, struggling physician. Can you wonder that it could terminate only in one way?

"I accepted him, and by the time that you are reading this we shall be married and far away. So good-bye, Harry. Try and forgive me, if you can.

"IRIS."

With a horrible imprecation, Kendal tore the note into a thousand fragments, hurled them upon the floor, and ground his heel into them.

"False!" he cried. "I might have known it. It is always these beautiful women who are so heartless. They draw men on with their smiles and their bewitching fascinations, only to throw them over when a more eligible *parti* appears upon the scene."

Deeply as he had been smitten with her charms, her action caused an instantaneous revulsion of feeling.

"'What care I how fair she be, if she be not fair to me?'" he cried out, bitterly, to himself. "What a fool I was, to be duped by her so long! The iron has entered deep into my soul, but she shall see that she can not quite crush me. I will live to be revenged upon Iris Vincent if it costs me my life! If Dorothy inherits the million, I will marry her before the sun sets to-night. I only wish that I had known the way that affairs were shaping themselves. I—I should not have treated Dorothy so harshly."

It seemed as though all in an instant his heart went back to her in the rebound.

He rushed hurriedly down into the dining-room, there to be met by Mrs. Kemp, who advanced toward him with a white, startled face.

"Oh, Mr. Kendal," she gasped, breathlessly, "you can never in the world guess what has happened!"

"I rather think I can," retorted the young man, harshly: "your niece, Miss Vincent, has eloped with the millionaire's son across the way."

"That—that is not what I had reference to," said Mrs. Kemp, with a sob. "I—I admit that Iris has eloped, but it is not she whom I meant, but Dorothy."

"What of her?" cried Kendal, sharply, little dreaming the truth.

Chapter XXIII.

For an instant Kendal looked at the housekeeper in amazement.

"What of Dorothy?" he repeated, breathlessly.

"She has disappeared too!" returned the housekeeper, faintly, adding: "She did not go with Iris, as you may imagine."

"No?" he echoed, faintly, inquiringly.

"No," she responded; "she went alone. She said to Katy, last night, 'If you wake up on the morrow, and do not find me here, do not weep. I shall be where I will be better off. No one will miss me—no one will know or care whither I have gone.' Katy thought them idle words, and paid little heed to them; but this morning, when she awoke and found that Dorothy was not in her room, in the greatest of alarm she came to me and told me what had occurred. At that moment I was just smarting under the blow of Iris' elopement, and words fail to describe my feelings at this second and most terrible catastrophe, for I realized how it would affect you, my poor boy."

Kendal had sunk down into the nearest chair, white as death, and trembling like an aspen-leaf.

He could hardly grasp the meaning of her words. "Dorothy gone—Iris fled with another!" His lips twitched convulsively, but he uttered no sound.

"I made diligent search for Iris and Dorothy," Mrs. Kemp went on, tearfully. "I found my niece had been married at the rectory, and had taken the first train to the city with her newly made husband; they intend starting on the steamer which leaves New York for Europe to-day. So, of course, there was nothing to be done in Iris' case, so I turned my attention to Dorothy. But, as I remarked before, it was useless. I think she must have gone to New York City, and if she has, trying to find her will be like hunting for a needle in a hay-stack. I was shocked that she should have left to-day, because she well knew that this was the day on which the will was to be read, and that concerns her so vitally. Ah! here is the lawyer now," and before Kendal could frame a reply the gentleman was ushered into the old-fashioned library.

He greeted both Mrs. Kemp and the young man gravely, and they knew by his demeanor that he had heard what occurred.

His very first words assured them of that fact, and he went on to say that Dorothy's disappearance, however, would make no difference in the reading of Doctor Bryan's will, which was set for that day and hour.

"As my time is rather limited," he continued, "you will, I trust, pardon me if I proceed to business at once."

He looked sharply from one to the other, and, as they both bowed assent, he opened the satchel he had brought with him, and proceeded to take out the document which meant so much to Kendal, unfolded it with great precision, and in his high, metallic voice he read it through slowly and impressively.

Kendal had quite imagined that the old doctor would leave him a goodly share of his vast estate—perhaps something like a hundred thousand or so—indeed, he would not have been surprised to have learned that the doctor had left him a quarter of a million dollars.

To his unspeakable horror he found that he had been cut off without a dollar; all had been left to Dorothy, without reserve or condition, save one, and that condition was a most important one: that she should marry Kendal six months after his decease, or relinquish the fortune bequeathed to her.

"I may as well explain to you my old friend's idea in making this will," said the lawyer, turning to the young man. "He wished Miss Glenn to marry you, and thought this the most expedient and effectual way of bringing about the marriage of two young people whose interests he had so deeply at heart. Had he lived long enough to have made a new will, I am sure it would have been entirely different."

But not one word of all this did Harry Kendal hear. His brain was on fire. He only realized one thing—that he was a beggar on the face of God's earth; and, to make matters worse, he had by his own rash act driven Dorothy from beneath that roof, thereby cutting off his own chance of marrying her and being master of Gray Gables.

He clinched his hand and ground his handsome white teeth together in terrible rage.

There was but one thing to do, and that was to find Dorothy ere the fortnight waned, and marry her at once—that is, if he could ever persuade her to forgive him.

He had parted from her in bitter anger, and said words to her that women never forgive when uttered by those whom they love. The worst part of the whole affair was, their quarrel had been over another girl.

"No steps will be taken until the fortnight has elapsed," said the lawyer in his metallic voice; "and at the expiration of that time, if we do not congratulate you, Mr. Kendal, upon your marriage to Miss Dorothy, we shall have to make great changes at Gray Gables. Allow me to wish you both a very good-morning."

With these brief words the brisk little lawyer took a hasty departure.

Mrs. Kemp and Kendal stood looking at each other long after his departure with faces pale as death.

It was the housekeeper who broke the silence.

"I am sorry for you, Mr. Kendal," she said. "It is a terrible thing to have one's hopes dashed after that fashion—and when one doesn't deserve it, either. You were always so good and faithful and true to Dorothy, sir; even keeping your promise with her through the most terrible affliction that ever could have befallen her—that of blindness. It is dreadful to think that the moment she regained her sight, and believing herself to be the possessor of a great fortune, that she should show every one so plainly that she thought you were not good enough for her to marry by running away from you, Mr. Kendal!"

Every word she so innocently uttered cut him like a sharp sword.

"Not good enough for her?" he echoed, crushing back the imprecation that sprang to his lips. His blood boiled at the construction which she put upon the matter. It was a terrible blow to his pride, yet he dared not utter the truth until he should know whether or not he should be able to find Dorothy and marry her within the allotted fortnight.

Without a word Kendal turned on his heel and quitted the room, slamming the door after him with a decided bang.

Before the sun set that night he was in New York City again and searching for Dorothy.

It meant a fortune for him. He *must* find her. He dared not think of what failure would mean to him—of the ruin that would stare him in the face.

The idea suggested itself to him that in all probability Dorothy would seek out her old companions of the book-bindery. He felt that it would be rather daring to go there, where he would meet Nadine Holt, after his so abrupt desertion of her; but his anxiety over Dorothy overcame all scruples, and late that afternoon the girls of the Hollingsworth book-bindery were astonished at the door being flung suddenly open and seeing the handsome young man whom they had known as the street-car conductor and Nadine Holt's lover standing on the threshold.

His eyes ran rapidly over the scores of girls at their tables, resting at length upon a fair, pale thoughtful young girl standing nearest him. He remembered having often seen her with Dorothy. He recollected, too, that her name was Nannie Switzer. He stepped up to her and raised his hat with that courteous bow that was always so fascinating to young girls.

"I beg your pardon," he said, "but, finding myself in your vicinity, I dropped in to look up my old friend. I refer to the young girl with whom I used to see you so much—Dorothy Glenn."

To his utmost surprise, the young girl burst into a flood of tears.

"Oh, sir, you can not tell how your words affect me!" she sobbed.

"Why?" he asked, surprisedly.

The girl hung her pretty head, and her blue eyes sought the floor in the greatest embarrassment.

"Will you tell me why?" he repeated, earnestly. "It is my right to know, is it not, Miss Nannie?"

"Well, you see, sir," she stammered, confusedly, "we have not seen or heard anything from Dorothy Glenn since Labor Day and every one hereabouts thought that—that *you* knew where she was."

He flushed a dark crimson and gave a guilty start.

"I am so glad to know that our suspicions were groundless," she breathed, thankfully; adding: "I am indeed sorry that I can not tell you where Dorothy is; we would all give the world to know, I assure you."

He could not help asking next, in a low, husky voice:

"What of Nadine Holt? Where is she?"

Again the girl's face clouded.

"She has worked right along here with us up to a week ago," she answered, "and then Nadine went away suddenly, without saying so much as good-bye to any of us." She could not help but add: "She has changed so greatly that you would never know her. She is no longer the dark-eyed beauty whom you remember; she looks ten years older. She never smiles now, and there is a horrible look in her eyes—like the cunning gleam one sees in the eyes of the insane; and, oh! sir, let me warn you—*you*, of all men—for the love of Heaven, do not cross her path! Remember, I—I warn you."

Chapter XXIV.

Harry Kendal threw back his dark, handsome head with a gesture of disdain and looked at the girl.

"I do not know of any reason why you should warn *me*, above all other men, that it is dangerous to cross Miss Holt's path," he said. "Almost any young man will flirt with a pretty girl when he finds her so *very* willing. She understood that it was only a flirtation; but when I met your little friend Dorothy, of course all that nonsense with Nadine ceased."

"Nadine did not call it a flirtation," returned the girl, gravely. "You might call it that. She thought of it differently, I am sure."

"Where is Jessie Staples?" he asked, abruptly, to change the embarrassing subject.

"She, too, has left the bindery," was the unexpected reply. "There have been great changes among the people in this book-bindery within the last few months. A young man connected with the place had quite a sum of money left him, and Jessie Staples was a great favorite with this young man's mother, so at their invitation Jessie went to live with them."

Finding that she had nothing more to tell him, Kendal soon after took his departure.

He was desperate as he walked along the street.

"What in the name of Heaven shall I do?" he cried. "One day of the fortnight has already passed, and I have not even the slightest clew to Dorothy's whereabouts." And in that hour in which he realized that she was indeed lost to him he knew how well he actually loved the girl. Iris' fickleness had killed his mad infatuation at one blow, and, man-like, his heart returned at once to its old allegiance.

Now that he knew that it was only a question of the merest chance of ever finding Dorothy, his very soul seemed to grow wild with anxiety.

Suddenly a thought born of desperation occurred to him—why not consult a fortune-teller as a last resort? It just flashed across his brain, an advertisement he had read and laughed over in one of the New York papers a few days before:

"Madame ———, seventh daughter of the seventh daughter, reveals to those who wish to consult her all the main incidents of their past, present, and future life; brings together the hearts of those who are suffering from the pangs of lovers' quarrels, though the whole wide earth should separate them; indicates the whereabouts of missing ones, though they should be hidden as deeply and securely from sight as the bowels of the earth. The madame can with ease secure for you the love of any person whom you may choose to win, put each and every person in the way of making fabulous fortunes in the shortest possible space of time, and all this for the small sum of fifty cents. Madame can be found, between the hours of nine and twelve in the forenoon, one and six in the afternoon, and from seven until eleven in the evening, by those who wish to consult her marvelous powers, on the fourth floor of the last tenement house on Hester Street. Visitors will please take note that Madame's consultation studio is in the rear of the building. A candle lights the way."

By dint of much perseverance Kendal found the place.

Taking the candle, he groped his way through the long, narrow, grimy passage, and found himself at length standing before Room 106, as the advertisement had indicated.

His loud, impatient knock was answered, after some little delay, by a tall figure hooded and cloaked, the face almost concealed by a long, thick veil that was thrown about the head, and which reached almost to the feet.

In a black-gloved hand this strange apparition held a lighted candle.

"I trust I have found the right place," said Kendal. "I am in search of Madame Morlacci, the fortune-teller."

At the sound of the deep, rich, mellow voice, the figure started back as though it had been struck a sudden blow, the black-shrouded hand that held the candle shook as if from palsy.

"Come in," replied a muffled voice, that sounded like nothing human, it was so weird.

Kendal stepped fearlessly into the room, the corners of which were in deepest gloom, which the flickering rays of the candle could not penetrate.

"Well," said Kendal, impatiently, "I should be grateful to commence the preliminaries of this fortune-telling business at your earliest convenience, if you please, madam; my time is somewhat limited."

Kendal drew forth his pocket-book, took out a bank-bill and handed it to the strange creature; but, to his intense surprise, she flung it back almost in his face.

"I can tell you all you wish to know without a fee," cried the hoarse, muffled voice, which somehow made every drop of blood in Kendal's veins run cold as he heard it.

"That would not be very profitable to you, I am sure, madame," he said, wonderingly.

"That makes no difference to you," was the almost rude answer. He felt quite disconcerted; he hardly knew what to say next. This certainly was an odd *contretemps*, to say the least. "You are here to learn the whereabouts of—a woman?" she whispered, in a deep, uncanny voice. "Is it not so?"

"By Heaven! you are quite right," cried Kendal, in amazement, quite startled out of his usual politeness.

This woman had never laid eyes on him before, he told himself. Now, how, in the name of all that was wonderful, could she have known this? He had sneered at fortune-telling all his whole life through; now he began to wonder if there was not something in it, after all.

"This woman, who is young, and by some called beautiful, will be your evil genius!" she hissed. "You wronged her through your fickle-mindedness, and wrecked her young life."

"Great God!" he cried, "are you woman or devil, or a combination of both? But go on—go on!" he cried, excitedly. "I see you know all my past. There is no use in my attempting to hide anything from you. But tell me, where shall I find this young woman of whom you speak? I must track her down."

A laugh that was horrible to hear broke from the lips of the veiled woman opposite him.

"That you will never be able to do!" she cried, fiercely. "Though she may cross your path at will, you might as well hunt for a particular grain of sand along the sea-shore, a needle in a haystack, a special blade of grass in a whole field. You may recognize this fact, and abide by it. But, hark you! listen to what I have to say: The fates have decreed that your heart shall be wrung as you have wrung hers—pang for pang!"

"Who and what are you," he cried, "who talk to me in this way? You act more like a vengeful spirit than a woman unconcerned in my affairs. Who and what are you, anyhow?"

"I tell you only what I see," was the muttered response.

"See where?" demanded Kendal in agitation.

"That is not for you to know."

"But I shall—I will know!" he cried, furiously. "There is something underneath all this trumpery. I am not a man to be trifled with in this fashion, I can tell you, with your fortune-telling nonsense—humbuggery!"

"Then, pray, what brings you here? what is your object in coming?" asked the other, with a covert sneer.

"To hear what lies you could trump up," replied Kendal boldly.

"Our interview is ended," said the veiled figure, rising and pointing her long arm toward the door.

He knew that he must temporize with her if he would find out Dorothy's whereabouts, which he was beginning to believe she might find out for him.

"Will you pardon me?" he asked, humbling himself. "I—I must know more."

"You have heard all that I have to say, Harry Kendal!" she cried.

Who was this creature who knew him—aye, knew his name, his most secret affairs? He must—he would know.

With a quick bound he cleared the space which divided them, and in a trice he had grasped her wrists firmly and torn the veil from her face.

This was followed by a mighty cry.

Chapter XXV.

The instant Harry Kendal sprang toward the veiled woman she sprang backward, as though anticipating the movement, and quick as a flash she overturned the candle, just as he tore the veil from her face.

A low, taunting laugh broke from her lips through the inky darkness of the room. In a trice she had torn herself free from his grasp, and like a flash she had sped from the room and down the narrow hall and stairway, like a storm-driven swallow, leaving her companion stumbling about the place, and giving vent to curses loud and deep as he fumbled about his vest pocket for matches.

The veiled woman never stopped until she reached the street, then paused for a moment and looked back as she reached the nearest gas lamp.

As the flickering rays of the street lamp fell athwart her face, the features of Nadine Holt were clearly revealed, her black eyes blazing, and her jet black hair streaming wildly about her face.

"How strange!" she panted, "that this idea of fortune telling should have come to me as a means of gaining my living! I was driven to do something. And that he should have been the very first patron to come to me—he, of all others! He is tracking me down because I maimed the girl whom he is so soon to wed—yes, tracking me down to throw me into prison—and yet he was once my lover! It is always the way. When a man's heart grows cold to one love, and another's face has charmed him, it seems to me as though men have a cruel, feverish desire to thrust the first love from them at whatever cost. But I will be revenged upon him! I will live to make his very life a torture; but I shall do it through Dorothy Glenn. I will go to Dorothy Glenn at once, and we shall see what will happen then."

Meanwhile, after much fumbling and imprecations loud and deep, Kendal succeeded in striking a match and finding the overturned bit of wax taper, which he hastily lighted, peering cautiously into the inky darkness which surrounded him.

He was tired and exhausted, and he told himself that he would turn in at the nearest hotel, take a good night's rest, and mature his plans on the morrow for finding Dorothy.

Meanwhile, let us go back, dear reader, to the hour in which our heroine, little Dorothy, decided to leave Gray Gables.

For some moments after Harry Kendal had left her in anger in the corridor she stood quite still—stood there long after the sound of his footsteps had died away, trying to realize the full purport of his words—that their engagement was at an end, and that they had parted forever.

The whole world seemed to stand still about her. Then, like one suddenly dazed, she turned and crept into her own room. Katy was there awaiting her.

She suffered the girl to place her in a chair, to take the faded blossoms from her hand and from her corsage, to unfasten the strings of pearls, and to remove her ball dress.

By degrees she had informed Katy of her regaining her sight, and the poor girl's joy knew no bounds.

She wondered greatly how Dorothy could feel so downcast in such an hour, and she never once heeded Dorothy's sad words—that she was going to leave Gray Gables before the dawn, as there was no one there who loved her.

It was so late when Katy sought her own couch that she soon dropped into a deep sleep. This Dorothy had watched for with the greatest impatience. She soon rose, robed herself in a dark dress and Katy's long cloak, and was soon ready for the great undertaking which she had mapped out for herself.

Hastily writing a note, she placed it where Katy's eyes would be sure to fall upon it early the next morning; then she stole quietly from the room. The great clock in the corridor below struck three as she passed it with bated breath and trembling in every limb.

She opened the door softly and stole out into the chill, raw night.

There was no one in this wide world to miss her, no one to care what became of her! She was in every one's way. Only one thought suggested itself to her—to end it all. Perhaps Harry Kendal would feel very sorry when the news came to him on the morrow that she was dead—she whom he had spurned so cruelly only the night before. And perhaps he would throw himself beside her cold, dead body and wish that he had been less cruel to her, and cry out:

"Oh, if God would but roll back His universe and give me yesterday!"

She had no fixed destination, but walked on and on, until she suddenly found herself down by the Yonkers Boat Club House, that stretched its dark shadow afar out into the river. It was connected with the shore by a long, narrow plank walk.

Mechanically Dorothy crept down the narrow, winding stairway that led to it. Midway on the plank walk she paused, clung desperately to the rail and looked fearfully down into the dark, flowing river that rushed on so madly but a few feet below her.

Only a few flickering stars would see and know all, she told herself. There would be but a plunge, a deathly shiver as her warm body came in contact with the icy waves, a moment of choking, a terrible sensation, then all would be over—her troubles would be at an end!

What cared she for the wealth of a hundred Gray Gables and princely estates when love's boon was denied her?

Even in that hour and in that weird place she thought of the words another heart-broken girl had uttered long years before:

"You have learned to love another,You have broken every vow;We have parted from each other,And my heart is lonely now.

"Oh! was it well to severThis fond heart from thine forever?Can I forget thee? Never!Farewell, lost love, forever!

"We have met, and we have parted,But I uttered scarce a word;But, God! how my poor heart startedWhen thy well-known voice I heard!

"Oh! woman's love will grieve her,And woman's pride will leave her;Life has fled when love deceives her,Farewell—farewell forever!"

"I am so young to die!" sobbed Dorothy. "I haven't done very much good in the world, but surely I have done no wrong."

Then it occurred to her suddenly—a little trifle which she had quite forgotten:

She had taken Nadine Holt's lover from her, and the girl was broken-hearted over his loss; and now Heaven had, in turn, taken him from her. This was God's vengeance upon her.

Could even Nadine Holt see her now she would feel sorry and find pity for her.

Suddenly, to her intense amazement, Dorothy saw a man hurrying along the high cliff just above where she stood. He was advancing toward her with hasty strides that broke almost into a run.

Dorothy noticed that he carried a large black bundle in his arms, and that he was heading directly toward the boat house.

She saw him lean forward, raise the bundle quickly and dash it into the river, turn rapidly, and break into a quick run in the opposite direction.

The bundle did not quite reach the water's edge, she saw; he had missed his aim.

Dorothy stopped short and peered over the rails at it, wondering what it could contain.

As she did so she observed that there was motion within the small, dark bundle. It contained some living thing, she felt quite sure.

Dare she go and examine it? she asked herself. Perhaps it was some poor animal doomed to death that was bound up in that unsightly bundle.

Her heart stirred with pity at the thought, and at that moment a cry, faint and muffled, broke the stillness of the night.

It emanated from the dark bundle. Quick as a flash Dorothy retraced her steps until she reached the bank, and down this she clambered with alacrity.

But when she was almost within reach of the bundle it rolled down into the water with a splash, and the mad waves covered it.

With a cry Dorothy sprang forward just in time, and caught it as the undertow was bearing it out into the deep water.

Again there was a quick cry and struggle within the bundle. In a twinkling Dorothy had torn off the wrappings.

"Oh, God in Heaven!" she cried, "it is a little child!"

Chapter XXVI.

The cry died away in Dorothy's throat as her terrified eyes fell upon the bundle which she held in her arms.

Yes, it was a little child.

"Oh, the cruelty of it!" she sobbed aloud. Some one had doomed it to death on this bitter night, and she thanked Heaven for bringing her to that spot to save its life.

Wrapping it quickly in the ends of her long thick cloak, Dorothy hurried to the nearest shelter with it.

This happily proved to be a small cottage on the outskirts of the town. A solitary ray of light shone from one of the windows, and without hesitation Dorothy hastened up the little narrow path to the porch and rang the bell.

She quite believed that she would know the inmates of the cottage, for she well knew every one in the village.

It was a strange woman that opened the door at length and peered out at her, and a shrill voice cried:

"Why, as I live, Maria, it's a woman standing out here with a child in her arms! Why, what in the world can you want?" she cried, addressing Dorothy.

"I thought I should see some one here whom I knew," faltered Dorothy.

"No; we are strangers here," replied the woman. "We have just moved into this cottage to-day. We are from down country, my man and me, and my girl Maria. We don't know any one hereabouts, so I can't direct you. But, dear me! it's an uncanny time of night for a woman to be out. You ought to be careful of your little baby, if you have no thought for yourself, ma'am."

Dorothy tried to speak, but words seemed to fail her.

"But won't you come in and rest for a bit?" asked the woman, pityingly. "I can't let you go away without at least warming yourself by the fire. I am sitting up with my sick daughter."

Dorothy gladly accepted the kindly offer and entered.

Dorothy was about to tell the woman the story of how she had rescued the little one, when it occurred to her that this would necessitate her explaining how she herself had come to be in that locality at that hour, and this she shrank from doing.

The woman was a stranger in the neighborhood, she argued to herself, and would never know her again. Why not hold her peace? But, then, what would she do with the little one that Fate had thrown so strangely upon her mercy?

She quite believed that it did not belong to any one in the neighborhood, nor had she heard of a little one like this. She saw that the clothing upon it was of the daintiest texture, and the embroidery upon it was of the finest.

"Oh, what a beautiful little baby!" cried the woman, her heart at once warming toward the little stranger. "How much it looks like you!" she added, turning to Dorothy.

"What!" cried the girl, in amazement.

"I said your baby looked like you," repeated the woman.

She wondered why the young girl flushed to the roots of her golden hair.

"We must go now," said Dorothy at length; "and I thank you, madame, for your hospitality."

The woman, with clouded eyes, looked after the slender figure as it disappeared.

"A lovely but very mysterious young woman!" she ejaculated. "I hope everything is all right. She is so very young. It is a great pity for the little child."

Meanwhile, Dorothy struggled on through the dim light of the fast dying night, and soon found herself at the railway station without any seeming volition of her own.

In her pocket was her purse, which the good old doctor in one of his generous moods had filled to overflowing. She had had no occasion to use it until now.

The poor little one had commenced to cry now, and when Dorothy hushed its cries it cuddled up to her with a grateful sob and nestled its head on her arm.

Why shouldn't she keep the baby that fate had sent directly into her arms? she asked herself?

Yes, she would keep it. For was there not a bond of sympathy between this poor little one, whom those who should have loved and cared for had consigned to a watery grave, and herself, who had sought the same watery grave to end her own wretched existence?

"You and I will live for each other, baby," she sobbed, holding the wee mite closer. "I will keep you for my very own, and I will pray for the time to come when you will be big enough for me to tell you all my sorrows. You will put your little arms around my neck and your soft, warm cheek against mine, and try to comfort me."

Dorothy had made her resolve, little dreaming that it would end in a tragedy.

She boarded the train, and was soon steaming away toward New York city—the great, cruel city of New York, rampant with wickedness and crime.

More than one passenger noticed the lovely young girl with the tiny infant in her arms, and marveled as to whether or not it could possibly belong to her; for surely the girl could not be a day over sixteen, or seventeen, at most.

All unconscious of this close scrutiny, Dorothy watched the little one with wondering eyes all the way until she reached the metropolis.

Her first idea was to seek a boarding place, and then she could look about her.

To her dismay, among the half score to which she walked until she could almost drop down from exhaustion, no one cared to take her and the child in; and it seemed to her, too, that they were rude in refusing her, and more than one actually shut the door in her face.

She was tired—so tired—carrying the heavy child in her arms. She had given the name Miss Brown to each instance, and at last one landlady came out bluntly and said to her:

"It would sound a deal more proper to call yourself Mrs. Brown, if you please, ma'am," at the same time pointing to the child in her arms.

Then it dawned upon Dorothy's mind why every one had refused them shelter, even for money.

"Why shouldn't I call myself Mrs. instead of Miss Brown? One name is as good as another," she said to herself. It was all the same to her; anything, so that she would not be separated from this poor little baby, whom she had learned to love in those short hours with all the strength of her yearning heart.

At the next boarding house, recklessly enough, Dorothy gave the name of Mrs. Brown, and she found no trouble in securing accommodations there.

"Poor child! she seems so young to be left a widow!" exclaimed the landlady, in relating to her other boarders that night that she had let room sixteen to such a pretty young woman, with the loveliest little angel of a baby that ever was born.

No one ever yet took a false position without finding himself ere long hedged in with difficulties.

And so poor Dorothy found it.

She was continually plied with questions by the rest of the boarders as to how long since her husband had died, and how long since she had taken off mourning, or if she had put on mourning at all for him, and if baby reminded her of its poor, dear, dead papa.

Dorothy's alarm at this can more readily be imagined than described. She almost felt like bursting into a flood of tears and running from the room.

It had gone so far now that she was ashamed to tell the truth; and then there was the terrible fear that if people knew it was not her very own they would take it from her; and she had learned to love it with all the fondness of her desperate, lonely heart.

And then, too, it seemed to know her and feel sorry for her.

It knew her, and would coo to her, and cry for her to take it.

She had named it, long since, little Pearl, because she had fished it from the water. But, to tell the truth, she found it a terrible responsibility on her hands.

She did not know what to do with the child.

She could not go out and leave it in the house, and she couldn't take it with her.

She had been searching for a situation the last few days, and, to her unspeakable horror, she found that no one wanted a young woman encumbered with a child.

Had she been older, she would have known better than to have assumed such a responsibility; but Dorothy was young, and had some of life's bitterest lessons yet to learn.

Dorothy had turned her face resolutely against the fortune which Doctor Bryan had left.

She quite believed, if she was not there to receive it, it would go to Kendal, her faithless lover.

She wanted him to have it. She did not care for any of it.

She had been only a working girl when Doctor Bryan sought her out and took her to his home; she could be only a working girl again.

Chapter XXVII.

In the hour of Dorothy's desolation her heart went back to Jack Garner, who had loved her so in other days. Poor Jack! whom she had thrown over so cruelly for a handsomer, wealthier fellow, only to be deserted by him in turn for the first pretty face that had crossed his path.

And that very day came the turning point of her life.

She had answered an advertisement a few days before by letter to an intelligence office, and in the course of a week she received the following reply:

"MY DEAR MADAM—Replying to your note, would say your communication was hardly explicit enough for us to determine whether you would suit our patron or not.

"The party we refer to is Mrs. Garner, a widow. Her family consists of one son, a niece who lives with them, and a young lady.

"They wish a companion for Mrs. Garner. She requires a somewhat elderly woman. Even the child would not be so objectionable, if the right person were secured."

The letter dropped from Dorothy's hand, and she uttered a low cry; but presently picking it up, and reading it eagerly through again, she found a postscript added to it which read as follows:

"Call, if you please, at the Garner homestead to-morrow, at 10:30 A. M., if convenient."

Dorothy's heart beat quickly. Could it be possible that this Garner family and the one she had known were one and the same? Oh, no! it could not be, for they were poor, very poor, and these people lived in a fashionable quarter.

Jack might plod along all his life and never have a dollar ahead. Poor Jack! And her eyes grew moist as she thought of him. Ah, how well he had loved her!

Dorothy knew quite well that according to the requirements of the advertiser she would not suit on account of her youth. An older person than herself was wanted; yet the thought of the possibility of taking little Pearl with her caused her to ponder over the matter very carefully. Surely there was *some* way to meet the difficulty.

"I am afraid I will not get the situation I was telling you of last night," said Dorothy to her landlady; and she told her why.

"Youth and beauty, although the greatest blessings Heaven can give us, often bring with them a certain train of disadvantages. I once knew a young and most lovely girl who, on this very account, could not get work. She resorted to a desperate measure, but it insured success. Perhaps it might in *your* case. She put on, over her golden curls, a dark wig with plenty of gray in it, seamed a wrinkle or two under her long lashes with a camel's hair pencil, and put on a pair of glasses. She secured a position as housekeeper in an eccentric old bachelor's family, which consisted of only himself and his aged parents. Well, the old folks soon passed away, the old bachelor soon following them, and every dollar he had on earth he left to his housekeeper, to 'keep her from the poor house to which she would soon have to go in her old age,' as he phrased it. It was a large fortune, and she is enjoying it to-day with a young husband and dear little children gathered about her, and she often speaks of it when I see her, and tells me all her good luck came from putting on that wig, donning the spectacles, and lining her face to make it look old. She never would have gained that position otherwise, for she was very fair and childish in appearance."

"I think I will do the same thing!" cried Dorothy, enthusiastically. "It can do no harm, anyway. It is a terrible deceit to practice, but if I secure the position, and the people learn to like me, in a very short time I will reveal the truth to them, and I think they will find pardon for me and keep me in their employ."

"I am sure they will," assented her companion, "and all I can say is, I hope you may have as great good luck as the girl I told you about."

Dorothy smiled faintly.

"I—I would never care to be—be rich," she faltered. "There are some people whom Heaven intended to always work for a living—I am one of them."

"If you think of buying a wig, I have one to sell you," said the landlady. "I used to be in the theatrical business, and had all those things. I will show you how to make up for a middle-aged woman, so that even your own folks wouldn't know you in broad daylight."

Dorothy was a little dubious upon hearing all this. She wondered if it was not to sell the outfit that the landlady had suggested all this. However, she passively placed herself in her hands, and the work of transformation began.

"Now, look!" exclaimed the landlady, at length. "What do you think of yourself now?" and she placed a hand glass before her.

Dorothy uttered a low cry. Could that face be her own at which she gazed in the mirror's depths? Was she the old woman represented there? And from the bottom of her heart she thanked God that it was only make-believe; that beneath it all her face was still young and fair, without the ravaging touch of Time's withering hand.

But it touched her heart keenly to see her little Pearl, whom she was learning to fairly idolize, shrink from her.

"I must, indeed, look greatly changed," she said, with a sob.

Hastily dressing the little one, and taking her with her, Dorothy wended her way to her destination.

She had always looked upon a little child much the same as a little girl admires a big wax doll. *Now* she was beginning to realize that a real live baby must be washed and dressed and fed and attended to; that it wouldn't go to sleep or keep awake when people wished; in short, she was beginning to understand that it could be a darling little nuisance at times, even to those who adored the dimpled bit of precious humanity the most.

Fairly panting with carrying so heavy a burden in her slender arms, Dorothy reached at length the avenue and number—a magnificent brown stone mansion in the center of the block.

With beating heart she ascended the steps and touched the bell.

A very polite servant answered her summons and ushered her into a spacious drawing-room.

"Madame will be with you presently, as she is expecting you," he said, indicating a seat.

Little Pearl commenced to cry, and Dorothy was at her wit's end to know what to do with her.

She was all flushed with nervousness by the time she heard footsteps in the corridor approaching the room.

An instant later the silken *portières* were swept aside by a white, jeweled hand, and a white-haired lady entered.

Dorothy rose to her feet, and caught her breath with a low cry that died in her throat.

The room seemed to whirl around her. She stood face to face with Jack's mother!

Dorothy had never seen her but once or twice before in those old days.

She remembered every lineament of her face perfectly, however. How could she help it, when Mrs. Garner bore such a striking resemblance to her fair-haired, handsome son? But she could not understand it; it almost seemed as if she was in a dream to find Mrs. Garner here surrounded by such elegance as this.

But before she could collect her scattered senses the lady advanced toward her, saying, in her sweet, kind voice:

"You are very punctual, Mrs. Brown. This is in itself a great recommendation. You are tired holding the baby in your arms. I will ring for one of the servants to relieve you for a little while, if you wish."

Dorothy never remembered in what words she thanked her, and she was even too confused to keep the thread of the conversation, but was conscious that she was replying at random. Yet the kind old lady did not seem to notice her confusion.

"I want some one for a companion," said the lady, slowly. "I have recently lost my niece, Miss Barbara Hallenbeck, and her death preys heavily upon my mind."

Dorothy was shocked at the news, but she could utter no comment.

"I am soon to lose my son," went on Mrs. Garner, slowly.

Dorothy sprang to her feet with a gasping cry:

"Jack dying!"

Poor, dear, faithful Jack Garner, who had loved her so well! It seemed to Dorothy that every pulse in her body quivered, and her heart was almost bursting at the news.

In that one hour the girl's heart was revealed to her.

She was face to face with the truth at last: she loved Jack Garner—yes, she loved Jack!

In that moment of time the past seemed to glide before her mental vision like a vast panorama.

She turned with a gesture of woe pitiful to behold to his dear old mother.

"You are about to lose your only son?" she gasped. "May Heaven pity you!" She was almost about to add: "If I could save his life by giving my own, oh, how gladly I would do it!"

Mrs. Garner saw the look on her face, and rightly interpreted it.

"Do not misunderstand me," she added, hastily. "I do not mean that I am to lose him by death. My son is soon to be married."

Chapter XXVIII.

For a moment the room seemed to whirl around Dorothy. The words seemed to strike into her very brain as they fell from Mrs. Garner's lips. "My son is soon to be married!" and the four walls seemed to repeat and re-echo them.

"I shall lose a son, but I shall gain a dear daughter," added the old lady, softly.

For an instant, as Dorothy sat trembling there, the impulse was strong upon her to fly from the house. The very air seemed to stifle her.

While she hesitated, fate settled the matter for her. The front door was opened by some one who had a latch-key, and a voice that thrilled every fiber of her being addressed some question to a servant passing through the corridor.

"Here is my son coming at last!" exclaimed the old lady, in pleased eagerness.

"Jack—Jack, my dear!" she called; "I am in the drawing-room. Step in a moment, my son;" and before Dorothy could collect her scattered senses the *portières* were parted by a strong, white hand, and Jack Garner stood on the threshold.

Ah! how changed he was in those few short months! The boyish expression had vanished. He looked older, more care-worn. The fair, handsome face was graver; the blue eyes were surely more thoughtful. Even his fair chestnut hair seemed to have taken on a deeper, more golden hue.

He crossed the room, bent over his mother, and kissed her.

"This is my son—Mrs. Brown, Mr. Garner," said the old lady, her voice lingering over the words with pardonable pride.

It was a terrible moment for Dorothy.

Would Jack know her? Would not those keen, grave, searching eyes penetrate her disguise?

He gave but a casual glance to the small, slim figure clad in black, and bowed courteously, then turned away.

The greatest ordeal of her life was past.

She had met Jack—Jack who had loved her so—face to face, and he had not recognized her.

She rallied from her confused thoughts by a great effort, for Mrs. Garner was speaking to her.

"I was saying, that as we seem mutually pleased with each other, we may as well consider the arrangement as settled between us."

Dorothy bowed. She could not utter a word in protest to save her life, although she had quite made up her mind not to remain under that roof.

"Your duties will be light, and I feel sure you will find ours a pleasant home. I will ring for one of the servants to show you to your room;" and suiting the action to the word, she touched the bell, and an instant later a neat little maid appeared, who courtesied and asked Dorothy to follow her.

"Madame will find her little child has already been taken to her apartments," said the girl, opening the door at the further end of the upper corridor.

Yes, little Pearl was there, cooing with delight at her new surroundings, and over the cup of hot milk and crackers on the little stand close beside her.

The girl rose hastily as Dorothy entered, set down the child, and quitted the apartment.

Upon finding herself alone with Pearl, Dorothy snatched the child up in her arms, sank down in the depths of a great easy-chair, and sobbed as though her heart would break.

"Oh, little Pearl! how I wish that we had never come here!" she moaned. "It makes me feel so sad."

The baby's blue eyes looked up into her own in wonder, but her soft cooing and the clasp of her little soft, warm fingers could not comfort Dorothy.

After luncheon she was called into Mrs. Garner's room.

"I am not feeling well," she said, motioning Dorothy to a seat. "I should like you to read to me until I fall asleep. Take any of the books from the book-case in the library. I have no choice."

The silent little figure in black bowed, and glided out of the room.

It was dusk in the library as she entered it, and while she pondered as to whether she should call some one to light the gas, to enable her to read the titles on the volumes, she heard Jack's voice.

But instead of passing, he entered, and proceeded to light the gas. With a beating heart Dorothy drew still further back, and at that moment another person entered the room.

"I knew I should find you here, Jack," said a voice that sounded terribly familiar to the figure in the window hidden by the silken draperies. "I have come to ask a little favor of you. I hope you will not find it in your heart to refuse me."

Before the last comer in the room had ceased speaking, Dorothy knew who it was—Jessie Staples!

A great lump rose in her throat, and her heart beat. She knew that she should have slipped from her place of concealment and quitted the room, but she seemed to have been held spell-bound by a power she could not control. She leaned heavily against the wall and listened with painful intensity to the conversation that was taking place between her old lover and Jessie, although she knew that it was wrong for her to do so.

"A favor you would ask of me?" repeated Jack, quickly. "Why, consider it granted beforehand," he returned, "if it is within my power."

"You are more than kind," murmured Jessie, adding: "The fact is, I have too painful a headache to attend the opera with you to-night, but I want you to go and enjoy yourself, and take some young girl in my place. I—I do not want to mar your happiness for this evening."

"I am quite sorry to seem unkind," he returned, "but really, Jessie, I beg that you will not ask me to take any one else to the opera, if you can not go. Although I promised beforehand, I trust you will not hold me to anything like that. I do not feel inclined to entertain any of your friends this evening, especially when you are not present. But, really, Jessie, I think it might do you good to go—the lights, and the music, and the gay throng, might divert your thoughts from yourself, and act as a wonderful panacea in banishing your headache."

"No—no!" returned Jessie; "believe me, I shall feel much better at home. But you must go. I could not forgive myself if I were to be the cause of your losing one hour of happiness, and I know, Jack, that you enjoy affairs of that kind so much. Go, if only to please me."

"If you are sure that it *will* please you, Jessie, I can not withstand your entreaties," he returned, thoughtfully. "Still, I have the hope that you may change your mind at the eleventh hour, and be ready to go with me," he added, laughingly. "I have a few letters to write, and will see you after I finish them. Remember it is not every night that one can hear Patti;" and with a few more pleasant words he quitted the room.

For some moments after he had left, Jessie Staples stood leaning against the mantel, gazing thoughtfully into the fire; then she was startled by a step close beside her.

She turned her head suddenly and saw a dark figure just leaving the room.

"Stay!" she called out; and the figure hesitated on the threshold. "Come here!" and the dark-robed figure advanced slowly and stood before her. "You are Mrs. Brown, the new companion?" she said, interrogatively.

"Yes," murmured a stifled voice.

"May I ask how long you have been standing in the room?" Miss Staples inquired, rather curiously. "I did not see you come in."

"I beg your pardon," came the faint answer. "I entered a few moments before you did, and when the gentleman entered and you commenced speaking, I—I hardly knew how to make my presence known, the conversation was so personal. I tried to make my escape from the room as soon as it was possible. I—I hope you are not angry with me."

"No," said Miss Staples, slowly. "I am sure the facts are as you stated them. You may resume your duties. That is all I wish to say," said Miss Staples.

Still the slight figure hesitated.

Poor Dorothy, how she longed to fling herself in Jessie's arms and cry out:

"Oh, Jessie, Jessie! don't you know me? I am Dorothy—your poor little friend Dorothy whom you used to love so dearly in the old days."

Still she dared not; no, she dared not betray her identity. And with one lingering glance she turned and slowly left the library, holding, tightly clutched in her hand, one of the volumes from the great book-case.

She had caught up the first one which she laid her hand on.

"You have been gone some time, Mrs. Brown," said Mrs. Garner, fretfully, as she entered the *boudoir*. "Let me see your selection. What book have you brought me? Why, as I live, it is the dictionary!" she exclaimed, in a most astonished voice. "Did you think I had need of that?"

The old lady flushed painfully. It was well known that it was one of her weak points to guard carefully from the world that she had no education whatever.

She would rather have died than to have let people know that she had at one time been a poor working-woman; and now this stranger, who had been only a hours beneath her roof, had discovered it.

She did not know what remark to make to Mrs. Brown, she was so aghast when the dictionary was handed her.

Chapter XXIX.

"You have made a very wise selection, Mrs. Brown," she said. "I quite agree with you that there is no book more instructive than the dictionary. You may read me twenty pages, or such a matter. I deem it very instructive, indeed—to you."

With a gasp, Dorothy took the book. Oh, how tedious it was, pronouncing word after word, and giving their definitions!

Every now and then Mrs. Garner would nod her head, remarking that such and such a word it would be well for her to take extra pains to remember, as they were in such general use in every-day conversation.

At length she ceased to make remarks altogether, and when Dorothy glanced up at her through the blue glasses which she wore, she found that the old lady was fast asleep, and with a very tired look on her face.

Dorothy laid down the book with a sigh, crossed her thin little white hands in her lap, and gave herself up to conflicting thoughts.

Only a little while before Jack had loved her so devotedly, and now he was about to marry Jessie, her friend of other days, whom he scarcely noticed when she was only Dorothy's friend.

While she was meditating over the matter, one of the maids put her head in at the door.

"If you please, Mrs. Brown, would you mind coming to Miss Staples a few moments?" she asked. "Her maid has leave of absence this week, and she misses her services."

"I will go with pleasure," said Dorothy, rising and following her at once.

As she entered the pretty blue-and-gold *boudoir*, she saw that Jessie had changed her mind about going to the opera that evening, for she was already dressed in opera attire.

"You wished to see me?" said Dorothy, in a husky voice.

"If you please, Mrs. Brown," said Jessie. "I should like you to accompany Mr. Garner and myself to the opera to-night, as my maid—that is, if Jack's mother has no objection, of course."

She did not catch the murmured words her companion uttered.

"There are a few little finishing touches to my toilet which I would like to have you help me with. In that velvet case on the center-table you will find a necklace of sapphires and diamonds. You may fetch it to me."

With trembling hands Dorothy clasped the necklace around Miss Staples' firm white throat.

"They are very beautiful—don't you think so?" she asked, looking at Dorothy with the old-time burst of enthusiasm which she remembered so well.

"Yes," returned Dorothy, in a low voice.

"They are Mr. Garner's gift to me. To-day is my birthday," she went on, "and this is Mr. Garner's gift—beautiful, is it not?"

"Yes," said Dorothy, in the same low, wistful voice.

"He is so considerate of my wishes; I had merely expressed the words that I admired sapphires and diamonds, and see! he has presented me with this lovely set!"

"The gentleman must have a very generous heart," said Dorothy, faintly.

Jessie Staples started and looked at her searchingly.

"Do you know that your voice reminds me of the voice of a young girl whom I once knew and loved dearly?" she said, huskily.

Oh, how those words thrilled every fiber of Dorothy's being!

"She was a very fair young girl," continued Jessie, thoughtfully, "but she went astray."

The bracelet that Dorothy was holding fell to the floor with a crash.

"Oh, I—I must have broken it!" she sobbed.

"Never mind," said Miss Staples; "you could not help it. Accidents are liable to happen at any time. It is not past mending, I am sure. Do not allow it to trouble you."

She quite believed that Mrs. Brown was a trifle awkward—probably a little nervous, and she did her best to reassure her.

"You must not feel badly about it," she repeated kindly. "I, too, am nervous sometimes. Why, only to-night I dropped my cup of chocolate, breaking the cup into bits, my hands were so nervous. I had such a headache all day, that I did not feel able to go down to the table. Even now I am by no means free from the terrible pain in my head. We shall leave the opera early," she went on, adding: "No doubt you are pleased to hear that."

"It does not matter much to me, madame," came the faint reply.

"The carriage will be here in half an hour. I trust you will be ready, Mrs. Brown. Please have my wraps in readiness then. One of the maids will tell you where to find them. You will not have much time to get your own wraps."

At the hour named, Dorothy stood ready, and a few minutes later Mr. Garner appeared in the corridor.

Taking Jessie's arm, he led her down to the carriage, seated her, helped in the little dark figure, and then proceeded carefully to tuck Jessie in with all the robes.

They were only ordinary attentions bestowed upon her companion, but they rankled deeply, like the thrust of a sharp sword, in the heart of the girl who sat there witnessing it all.

They talked upon indifferent subjects, but it seemed to Dorothy that every word held a double meaning.

Oh, how solicitous he was for her comfort! how he gathered the wraps about her, anxiously inquiring if she felt the cold air! how low and tender his words seemed to the girl sitting opposite them, and both seemed entirely oblivious to her presence.

The curtain was up when they reached their box, but all through the opera the little dark figure who shrank back behind the silken hangings saw nothing, heard nothing; she was watching so intently the old lover who was so near, and yet, alas! so far from her.

In the old days she had loved Jessie Staples, but now, as she saw her old friend and Jack Garner all in all to each other, she grew in a single hour to almost hate her for usurping her place in his heart.

True, there was not the same devotion that he had been wont to pay her; but then, Jack was older now and graver. How he had come by this sudden wealth puzzled her. Then, by degrees it all came back to her—how he used to say that some day there was a bare possibility of his being wealthy—-that he had some expectations from a distant relative. Surely those expectations must have been realized, or he could not be in the position which he was now enjoying. How strange that the Garners had lifted Jessie Staples out of the old life, and that she now was Jack's betrothed bride. And she wondered vaguely if he had forgotten the Dorothy he had loved so well.

Suddenly he turned toward her, and at that moment Jessie rose hastily to her feet.

"We will get home as quickly as possible," he said, hurriedly. "Miss Staples is indisposed."

Jessie leaned heavily on his arm, and they went quickly out of the building and into the carriage.

All the way home his arm supported her, and her head leaned helplessly on his shoulder.

Dorothy followed with her wraps up to Miss Staple's *boudoir*.

"Thank you—that will do," she said, wearily, dismissing her at her door, and Dorothy turned away.

One of the maids had rocked little Pearl to sleep, and the babe lay slumbering quietly in her crib.

Dorothy did not go toward it, as was her wont upon entering her room at night—indeed, she had forgotten about the child until she heard her cough, a little later on.

She was just about to cross the room to the little one, when one of the maids came hurriedly to her door.

"Would you mind sitting up with Miss Staples?" she cried, breathlessly; "she is anything but well. It looks to me as though she has a fever, but she will not hear to having a doctor called, or even of letting Mrs. Garner know how ill she is. She declares that, with a good night's rest, she will be all right in the morning."

Dorothy went hastily to Jessie Staples' room, while the girl remained to take charge of the child for the night.

She found Jessie as the maid had declared—quite ill and feverish-looking, but still wearing the soft chiffon dress she had worn at the opera, with the sapphire necklace gleaming on her white throat, and bracelets shining on her polished arms.

Dorothy went quickly up to her.

"You must let me remove these things, and get you into bed at once," she said coaxingly but firmly. "Your face is scarlet, and your hands tremble. You must take some hot lemonade, and go quietly to sleep."

Jessie was quite passive under her commands, but the pain in her head did not seem to abate.

For long hours, Dorothy worked patiently with her to allay the fever, but it seemed to increase with every moment.

She wanted to arouse the household, and send for a doctor, but Jessie pleaded most pitifully.

"You are very, very ill," cried Dorothy, in agony. "I must send for some one, or you will die!"

"Hush! I want to die!" cried Jessie, in a low whisper; "that is just it; I do not want to live."

Dorothy tried to soothe her, thinking it was but the idle vagaries of a wandering mind.

Chapter XXX.

"Hush!" cried Jessie, sinking back on her pillow, and clutching frantically the hand that held hers. "You must not call any one. I want to die! I am so tired of living. I want to tell you my story, Mrs. Brown—it seems to me that I shall go wild if I do not tell some one; and you seem so sympathetic and kind. May I trust you?" she whispered, with a great tremor in her voice.

"Yes," said Dorothy, slowly; "anything that you may say to me I will hold sacred."

"You are very good," returned the other. "You would think," she began, quickly, "that with wealth, and being the *fiancée* of a noble young man like Mr. Garner, and so soon to marry him, that I was the happiest girl in the world."

"Yes," returned the other, choking back a sob.

"I was not always surrounded by wealth and affluence, as you see me now," commenced Jessie Staples, burying her head in her pillow. "Only a few short months ago I was poorer than you are now, and worked for my daily bread. Among the companions who stood side by side with me was one, a lovely girl whom I loved with all my heart.

"She was gay and thoughtless, the life of the work-room, with her bright, girlish, mischievous pranks. Though they called her 'Madcap Dorothy,' yet every one loved her for her bright, winning ways.

"There was one employed in the same place whom I had loved ever since I could remember—loved in secret, making no sign, for it was hopeless—as he loved pretty Madcap Dorothy, and loved her with all the strength of his great, noble, manly heart.

"I was her best friend, even though she was in secret my rival. I did not care for myself. I only wanted to see the two whom I loved so well happy. One of them was Jack Garner, and the other Dorothy; and I will tell you of her."

"She was young, and gay, and pretty, as I have said, and she knew it. She knew that she had all of Jack's heart, but she longed for more heroes to conquer.

"One fatal day—oh, how well I remember it!—she fell in love with a handsome, black-eyed stranger—a car conductor on Broadway. That was the beginning of the end for Jack, who loved her so. One fatal day she ran away with the stranger and was never heard of again.

"Rumor has it that later on he tired of her, and was soon to lead to the altar a proud and lovely young girl—a school-girl—who had never known what it was to earn her bread, as did poor, pretty Madcap Dorothy.

"Dorothy's desertion nearly cost Jack Garner his life. I went and nursed him and took care of him; and when he recovered, his mother was stricken low, and I in turn nursed her.

"In the darkest hour of that terrible illness, when we were all gathered about her bedside, waiting for the angel of death to stoop and bear her away to that bright land that knows no grief nor partings, suddenly she beckoned Jack near her.

"'Oh, mother, is there anything that you wish?' he cried. 'Anything that I can do for you? Tell me if there is.'

"'Yes,' she whispered, 'there is one thing you could do, my son, that would make death easier to me. I—I could die happy if you would do as I ask.'

"'I promise you beforehand, mother,' he cried, 'if there is anything which I can do, it shall be done.'

"Feebly her hand crept toward mine and drew it toward Jack's, clasping them both together.

"'She has saved your life, my boy,' she whispered, 'and she has been as faithful as an angel to me—unto the last of mine. If you care for your mother's wishes, ask her to marry you, here and now. I love her as dearly as my life, Jack. My one wish in this world is to see you wedded to each other. You must say "Yes" or "No."'

"He buried his head in his hands, and I could see his stalwart form shake like a reed in a blast.

"He hesitated, but only for an instant. Slowly he raised his head, and I could see that his face was as white as death, in the dim-shaded light of the lamp. Then slowly he stretched out his hand toward me.

"'You know of my past, Jessie,' he said, huskily, 'and you know that my life-hopes were blasted. Will you take me under these conditions—if not for my sake, for—for my mother's?'

"I could not tell you the emotions that swept through my heart in that one moment of time.

"I do not know in what words I answered him; but, even without scarcely realizing what I did, my hand crept into his strong, cold one, and I nodded my head. I could not have spoken to have saved my life—my heart was too full for utterance.

"Mrs. Garner did not die that night, and she has always said ever since that she believed that promise brought her back from the gates of death to be a living witness to our happiness.

"Three months passed, with, oh! such unspeakable joy for me. My lover was all that a lover could be; still, there were times when I thought Jack's heart was not in his words, but was far away with the girl who had so cruelly jilted him.

"At length the wedding invitations were printed and sent out, and only a week later the terrible *dénouement* came that has shattered all my hopes.

"I was about to enter Mrs. Garner's *boudoir* one night, when I heard the sound of voices.

"Playfully I drew back, for I had recognized Jack's voice. I had a little gift for him, and I was hesitating a moment as to whether I should take it in and lay it on his lap, or wait until the next morning and give it to him in the library. Jack was pacing up and down, and I saw through the door, which was slightly ajar, that his face was very pale and stormy—and this was something unusual with calm, placid, courteous Jack.

"'For Heaven's sake, don't nag me any more, mother,' he cried, 'or you will drive me mad! Constant dripping will in time wear out even a stone. I have ruined my life to satisfy one of your whims; surely that ought to suffice. If I can't have peace in the house, I will take my hat and walk out of it. I can not endure this eternal nagging, that I must treat Jessie better—more as becomes a betrothed lover. You know very well that I do not love her. My marriage with her will be all your doing. My heart is with Dorothy; and when a man loves as I loved her, even if that love is destroyed, no one can ever fill the same niche in his affections. It is an impossibility. So, have done with this subject, mother, at once and forever.

"'I shall marry Jessie, because I am pledged to do so. I will make her life as happy as I can. She need never know that my heart is not hers, although she will bear my name.'

"I—I—never knew how I groped my way into an adjoining room," continued Jessie, "and there I sank down unconscious.

"How long I remained there I never knew. When I came to, Mrs. Garner, greatly frightened, was kneeling beside me and laving my face with eau-de-Cologne.

"And I knew by the fearful look in her eyes that she suspected that I had found out about Jack not caring for me.

"'Tell me what is the matter, my little Jessie!' she said, clasping me in her arms and pillowing my head on her breast.

"In broken gasps I told her, adding that I was going away—back to the poverty from which they had taken me, and Jack should never see my face again. Oh! how she prayed and pleaded with me on her bended knees, crying out:

"'If you love me, Jessie, do not break from Jack. I am sure he did not mean all he said. He was only incensed a little at me. He would not have you know it for the whole wide world. Oh, believe me, Jessie! Do not try to break my heart by your rash action. The marriage invitations have gone forth. What could we say to the people? Think of the scandal, Jessie, and save us from it. Let my words be a prayer to you. I am older than you are, Jessie. Let me tell you how this will be:

"'There might be in his heart only deep respect for you, but when he marries you, he will learn to love you. Every man loves his wife.'

"Against my own will and my better judgment, I allowed her to persuade me.

"I made no mention to Jack of what I had learned, but every day it has eaten into my heart like a worm in the heart of a rose.

"I loved him so well, I was only too willing to hold to him. I did not have the strength to follow the dictates of my own will; and now, God help me! the day is drawing nearer and nearer. What shall I do?

"My brain is going mad with the torturous thought that I shall stand at the altar by the side of a man who does not love me—whose heart is given to another.

"Every time that he stoops to kiss my lips I am sure he wishes they were hers.

"His thoughts are with her. I am a mere shadow to his life; she was the substance.

"People about me look upon me with envy, but you can realize that I am more to be pitied than the poorest beggar on the street. Tell me," she cried, eagerly, "do you think any one on this earth ever had a sorrow equal to mine?"

Chapter XXXI.

As the hours wore on, poor Jessie Staples grew so alarmingly worse, and the fever increased so rapidly, that, despite her entreaties, Dorothy felt that she must summon medical aid.

Soon after the entire household had gathered about Jessie, in the greatest alarm.

A physician was sent for at once—Doctor Crandall, whom Mrs. Garner had known for long years.

It so happened that the doctor lay very ill himself from an attack of *la grippe*, and, penning a line or so to Mrs. Garner, he explained that he had sent as a substitute a young doctor whom he had taken into his office to act for him during his illness. He felt sure they could rest Miss Staples' case with all safety in his hands.

That was the beginning of the terrible end.

Surely a cruel fate must have brought the situation about. It happened in this way:

When Harry Kendal had exerted every means to find Dorothy, and had failed, he commenced to look about for something to do.

It occurred to him that perhaps the best person to whom he could apply was Doctor Crandall, who had been the life-long friend of his old benefactor, Doctor Bryan.

Kendal's appeal was not in vain. He was taken in at once. Indeed, his coming was most opportune, he was told.

It so happened that his very first call was to the home of Mrs. Garner.

"Garner!" The name sounded very familiar to him. His brow darkened as he heard it. Was not that the name of the young man who had been Dorothy Glenn's lover when he first met little Dorothy in the book-bindery? Of course, it was absurd to imagine that there could be anything in common between these wealthy Garners and that poor fellow who worked hard at his trade. Still he hated the name.

When he reached the mansion and was ushered into the corridor, to his intense surprise, the first person whom he met face to face was Jack Garner! He recognized Jack at once; but the light in the corridor was low, and, besides, he had turned up his coat-collar, and with the heavy beard he had grown, Garner, as it was not to be wondered at, did not know him.

Besides, Jack had seen him but twice—once as he was putting Dorothy into a coach, and again on the Staten Island boat, in the dim, uncertain moonlight.

"Your patient is this way, doctor," he said, motioning him up the broad stairway.

A sudden, strange thought came to Kendal: What if he should find Dorothy there?

He no sooner entered the room and uttered the first word than the slim figure in black, wearing the blue glasses, started violently. Dorothy recognized him at once, despite the heavy beard.

"How in the world came he here?" she gasped to herself, in the greatest amazement.

But she had no opportunity to think long over the matter, for Jessie required the most immediate attention.

"I think it will be best to send you a practical nurse," he said, as he took his departure.

He spoke to Doctor Crandall about it immediately upon his return to the office.

"There is only one young woman whom I can think of just at present," said the doctor. "She is not what you might call a trained nurse, but she claims to have had a little experience. We shall have to secure her in a case of emergency. I shall send for her to-night; she will probably be there in the morning when you arrive."

As Kendal ascended the steps of the palatial home of the Garners, he came face to face with a woman who was standing in the vestibule, just in the act of touching the bell. One glance, and he fairly reeled back.

"Nadine Holt!" he cried, aghast, "is it you—*you*?"

"We meet again at last!" hissed the girl, confronting him with death-white face. "I knew I should find you sooner or later, and I have been on your track."

"Hush! hush! Nadine," he cried; "what do you mean? In Heaven's name, don't speak so loud! Every one is listening. You will ruin me."

"That is what I intend to do!" she shrieked, clutching frantically at his arm with her long, thin fingers. "You deserted me and wedded another."

"What put such a notion in your head, anyhow, Nadine?" he said, evasively, thinking it best to temporize with the raging fury confronting him.

"I heard all about it," she panted, hoarsely.

"Then some one has been cruelly maligning me," he cried; "and you, of all people in the world, Nadine, should not have believed it. Hush! some one is coming. I hear footsteps. Meet me later. I want to have a long talk with you. But, by the way, what are you doing here at this house, Nadine?"

"Did I not tell you that I answered Doctor Crandall's advertisement for a nurse, and that this is my errand here? But what are *you* doing here?"

"I may as well tell you the truth, Nadine," he said, despairingly, seeing that it would all come out sooner or later. "I—I have been studying medicine since I met you, and they have engaged me as physician. But now that surprises are in order, I suppose you know who lives here?"

"No," she answered.

"It is your old friend Garner, who used to be in the book-bindery. He has acquired sudden wealth—Heaven knows how. His mother is living with him, and also that pretty girl whom I used to think was so quiet—Miss Staples."

Before Nadine could reply, her amazement was so great, the door was opened by the quiet footman, and they were ushered into the drawing-room.

Kendal had barely time to whisper to Nadine: "These people do not know that I am the same one whom they used to know as the car conductor. Don't give me away," ere the door opened, and Mrs. Garner made her appearance.

"Ah! you have brought a nurse with you, doctor," she said, in a tone of great relief.

So saying, she led the way to the sick-room.

Nadine's entrance caused the greatest surprise to both Mr. Garner and Jessie.

No one thought of noticing the plain, dark little figure half hidden by the curtains in the bay window, or they would have seen Dorothy start and fairly gasp for breath as her eyes fell upon the nurse Kendal had brought with him, and heard them discuss the point that Nadine must be installed there as nurse.

Her brain fairly reeled, and it flashed over her mind what a villain Kendal really was.

She had quite believed all this long time that he had parted from Nadine Holt, and here he had been keeping up Nadine's friendship clandestinely through it all.

Of course Iris Vincent was expecting to marry him.

It was clear that Kendal had a good many irons in the fire.

She only wished that Iris Vincent knew of his friendship for Nadine.

Dorothy wondered if Nadine would penetrate her disguise.

Nadine assumed her duties at once, and the first thing which she did was to order the slim creature about, scarcely giving her a moment's rest.

Nadine had always heard that this was the way paid nurses invariably did.

She took every opportunity to consult Doctor Kendal and waylay him for long chats. Even Jessie noticed this, as ill as she was; and she noticed, too, that the young doctor resented it; and Nadine herself was not slow in perceiving his lack of interest in herself.

"How very interested you are in your pretty white-faced patient," Nadine said, on the second day of her stay there. "I almost believe you have fallen in love with Jessie Staples, and mean to bring her quickly back to health, and—and marry her."

Kendal turned from her with a fierce imprecation, and muttering something that sounded very like "the cursed jealousy of some women," abruptly quitted the room, slamming the door after him.

Then Nadine felt *sure* that she had stumbled upon the terrible truth.

Chapter XXXII.

Whenever a jealous woman is looking for something with which to feed the green-eyed monster, she usually finds it, or imagines she does, which amounts to the same thing. It was so with Nadine.

No one mentioned to Nadine the fact that Jessie was betrothed to Jack Garner. Even had she heard it, she would not have believed it. She would have imagined that it was a falsehood made up for her benefit.

She could not endure the kindly looks he gave Jessie, nor endure to see him bend over her, raise her from her pillow, and, while one strong arm supported her, coax her to take her medicine.

Such sights as these were more terrible for Nadine to endure than the pangs of death; and for hours afterward she would feel an almost uncontrollable desire to strangle the sick girl.

In Nadine's heart there rose a mad wish that Jessie would die before Harry Kendal became too fond of her.

While Jessie slept and she was not buried in the depths of a newspaper to kill time, she would be brooding over this subject: If Jessie Staples would only die!

One day, while in this morbid mood, her eyes fell upon a fatal paragraph that riveted her attention with breathless interest.

It spoke of the death of a once noted court beauty who had been in her time the toast of all Europe. Men had fought duels for her sake, and courtiers thought it a great honor to risk life and limb to do her bidding, being repaid by only a smile or one glance from her wine-dark eyes.

It happened that while riding about in her pony-cart she had, by chance, one day encountered a poor tradesman's son who had stopped by a brook at which her own horse was slaking his thirst, to give his steed a drink.

One glance at the fair, handsome Saxon face, and the girl who had laughed to scorn full many a lover, felt her heart going from her keeping to this bonny stranger.

Although he was poor—only a tradesman's son—and she had wealth untold, yet the beauty was not fair in his eyes.

He passed her by with only a gracious bow, as any courtier might, for he was in a hurry to reach the side of his beloved Gretchen. She was only a peasant maid, but in his eyes she was more beautiful than a queen.

He loved the pretty Gretchen with all his heart.

When my lady came to inquire about him, and learned he had a pretty little sweetheart, she grew very wroth, but she said never a word.

On that day she sent for Gretchen, and employed her as her maid. But from that hour there was a change in Gretchen's life.

Slowly but surely she faded, although her distracted lover did everything in his power to prolong the life of the maid he loved.

In the early spring-time, while robins sang and the trees put forth their blossoms, he gazed his last on all that was mortal of poor Gretchen.

The great lady tried her best to comfort Gretchen's lover, but he would not be comforted.

His hopes were buried in Gretchen's grave, and she could not turn his thoughts to herself, and ere the first moon waned, they laid him, too, beside his Gretchen, in his last home.

The great lady never smiled again, and soon after the doors of the convent closed upon one of the most beautiful women of her time.

On her death-bed she called one and all of those about her to listen to her tragic story.

She cried out that they must not touch her hand, for it was stained with human blood; and it was then that her horrible story was brought to light.

And in an awful whisper, while the long shadows deepened, she made this terrible revelation: that years, before she had murdered her maid, Gretchen, because the girl was loved by him whom she would have won.

By night and by day she pondered upon how it should be done, then suddenly the way and means occurred to her.

There was a powerful drug of which she had heard that gave women the most marvelous of complexions, but which sooner or later caused death.

Gretchen should take it; it could be placed in the basin of water in which she was wont to bathe her face each morning, and it would enter the body through the pores of the skin. In this way the doctors would be completely baffled, for they would not be able to trace the poison.

She put this dastardly plot into execution, and her cruel heart did not upbraid her, though she saw the girl droop and fade daily before her eyes.

When she looked out of her window and saw Gretchen and her lover pacing up and down the primrose path in the moonlight, a horrible laugh would break from the great lady's ripe, red lips.

"There will be but a few more of these meetings, tender partings and kisses under the larch-tree boughs."

She had never dreamed, this false, cruel beauty, that a man's heart could be constant to a dead love and spurn a living one.

All these years she had lived to rue it; but neither prayers, nor suffering, nor pangs of conscience could atone for the terrible crime committed.

During all the years that had passed since Gretchen had been lying in that lonely grave, she had never known one moment's peace of mind, until this hour when she lay dying and had confessed all.

Slowly, twice, thrice, Nadine Holt read the story through, and as she read, a terrible thought came into her own mind.

Why could not she procure this same drug and administer it in the same way to Jessie Staples?

She took the paper up to her room and hid it very carefully in her satchel.

True, Jessie had taken her in this time without saying one word of the past unpleasantness, treating her as though that quarrel had never been.

But Nadine was different. She was one of the kind that "never forgets, never forgives" while life lasts.

When the household was wrapped in deep sleep that night, Nadine stole out upon her terrible mission.

Several careful druggists refused to fill her order; but this did not daunt her. She knew that among the lot she would soon come across a catch-penny, and in this supposition she was quite right.

She soon found a place, and secured the deadly drug which she called for, and she stole into the house again without any one being the wiser for her midnight trip.

The light was burning low in the sick-room as she entered it, and Mrs. Brown sat half dozing in her chair by the bedside.

She started up as Nadine crossed the threshold.

"You needn't mind staying any longer," she remarked, brusquely; "I will take charge of the patient now."

"No," said the other, quietly but firmly. "It is between twelve and one that the most important medicine must be administered."

"Don't you suppose I am capable of giving it?" retorted Nadine angrily enough. "You don't seem to realize what is the business of a paid nurse!"

The other made no remark, but still she lingered. Had she a suspicion that there was anything amiss?

She was a strange creature, anyhow, with that old-looking face, the great mass of thick black hair studded with gray, and the thick blue glasses.

Where had she seen some one of whom this creature reminded her so strangely and so strongly?

Even the tone of her voice, although it sounded hoarse and unnatural, was somehow familiar to her.

The very way in which Mrs. Brown crested her head she had seen somewhere before, and it had made quite an impression upon her at the time.

"I can not help thinking that she is always spying upon every movement of mine, and she listens—I am sure she does—to every word the doctor and I say; and these people who watch others so much always need watching themselves."

Seeing that Nadine Holt was determined to banish her from the sick-room, Dorothy quitted the apartment with a very heavy heart, though she could not have told why.

Chapter XXXIII.

The days that followed were dark ones to the Garner household, for Jessie began to fail rapidly.

She grew so weak that the entire household began to grow terribly alarmed over her condition. Even the doctor had grave apprehension for his patient.

"The case of Miss Staples puzzles me completely," he said to Doctor Crandall, when he returned to his office one afternoon. "I have never known of symptoms like hers;" and he minutely described the strange turn the case had taken which had baffled him completely.

"As soon as I am able to be about I will go with you and see for myself just where the trouble is."

Meanwhile, a serious matter was agitating the brain of poor Jessie Staples.

She realized before any of the rest did that her condition was becoming alarming, and her wedding-day was drawing nearer and nearer.

But when that day dawned, a secret voice in her heart whispered that she would be "the bride of death," and not Jack Garner's.

She wondered if Heaven meant it for the best, that she must give up the life that might have held so much for her. She had longed for death many a time; but now that it seemed imminent, her very soul grew frightened because of one thought: she would have to leave Jack behind her. It seemed to her that though she should be buried fathoms deep, her soul would cling to earth—and Jack. What if, in time to come, he should forget her! Ah! that was the bitterest stroke of all; and she realized that, no matter how deeply a person may love, when the object of that affection dies, time brings balm to his woe, and mellows it into forgetfulness or to a shadowy memory.

If she were to die, would he ever love another, and stand with that other before the altar?

In her day-dreams, in times gone by, Jessie had pictured to herself—as girls will in those rosy moments—how she would stand at the altar, and listen with whirling brain and beating heart to those sweet, solemn words that would bind her forever to the man she loved with more than a passing love. She pictured how she would walk down the aisle, leaning on his arm—that great, strong arm that would be her support for evermore—a great mist of happy tears in her eyes as she clung to him.

She even pictured to herself how he would help her into the coach, and how they would drive away out into the great wide world together, to be separated never again.

Instead of all this, now she would be lying in her grave, with blue forget-me-nots and pale primroses on her breast.

Jack would be going through that scene with another as his bride; and as the years rolled by he would forget her, or think of her only now and then at times—not with keen regret, but with faint, vague indifference.

Oh, God! if it had been *he* who was destined to die, she would have shut herself up from the world, and would have lived only for his memory.

Her last prayer would have been, when death's dew gathered on her brow, to be buried beside him.

But men are more fickle than women. How few of them remain true to a dead love!

As she tossed to and fro on her pillow, these thoughts tortured her more than tongue could tell.

Then a strange fancy took possession of her.

The more she thought of it, the more her heart longed to accomplish it, until she could not restrain the longing that seemed to take entire possession of her.

And one day, when she seemed even more ill than usual, she could no longer restrain the impulse to send for Jack.

He came quickly at her bidding, sat down by her couch, caught the little white hand—ah! terribly thin and white now—in his, and raised it to his lips.

"Did you wish me to sit with you, Jessie?" he said. "Or would you like me to read to you?"

"No; I want to talk to you, Jack," she said, with a little quiver in her voice.

"Have you ever thought how near it is to—to our wedding-day, Jack," she whispered, faintly.

"Yes," said Jack, with never a thought of what was coming.

"What—what would you do if I were still ill when it dawned?"

"The ceremony could be performed just the same," he answered, promptly. "There would be no wedding at the church, no invited guests; that would be all the difference."

"Would you wish to marry me if—if you knew that I would never be well again, and that perhaps death would be hovering very, very near to claim me, and to part me from you?"

"I will keep to my part of the compact, Jessie," he said, huskily.

"But what if I should die before it, Jack?" she questioned, faintly.

"I do not know what you mean, Jessie," he said, gravely—"what you are trying to get at."

"Oh, Jack! I mean this: I—I want to belong to you in life and in death. I do not want you to have any other love but me, even if I should be taken from you. I want you to be true to me forever. I could not rest in my grave, though they burled me fathoms deep, if you ever called another—wife! If I am to die, Jack, you must promise me one thing—that you will never wed—another!"

"How can you talk of such a thing, my dear Jessie?" he said, reproachfully. "You pain me beyond measure."

"You will give me that promise, will you not, Jack?" she pleaded. "The pangs of death will be easier to bear if my mind is but at rest on that subject."

"You are going to get well soon, and the ceremony will take place as we have arranged," he said, soothingly; but she shook her head.

"If I should not, Jack," she whispered, fixing her burning eyes wistfully on his face, "let me have the assurance from your lips that you will never, never put another in my place."

"If it will settle any doubts in your mind, I give you the promise that you ask," he answered, in a low, grave voice; and it was worth that promise to see the girl's pale face light up with a swift flush of joy.

"Oh, thank you—thank you, Jack!" she sobbed.

At that moment a strange incident was taking place in Dorothy's room.

Almost thoroughly exhausted with night-watching, Dorothy had fallen asleep in a chair, in which she had sat down for a few moments' rest.

Was it only a vision? she wondered, or did she hear some one call her name softly: "Dorothy! Dorothy!"

She turned her head quickly, but she could see no one, although some one was whispering:

"Why do you nurse Jessie so carefully? If it is destined that she should die, I wonder that you grieve when you know that her death will bring freedom to Jack Garner and love to you!"

The idea was so startling that for a time it nearly took her breath away.

"Let her drift quietly on to the end which is near. If you do not work too zealously to save her, your reward will be the heart of him whom you *love at last*. Take warning, and heed my words!"

Dorothy sprang from her chair, quivering with excitement.

She had been fast asleep, and the words that still rang in her ears shocked her yet, even though she knew it was but a dream—though such a vivid one—and the voice that whispered those words to her seemed so like Jack's.

Still the idea was in her head. If Jessie Staples died, her lover would be free again, and she knew what that would mean for herself.

She tried to put the thought from her, but she could not; it haunted her continually.

She tried to tell herself that even if Jessie were to die, she would never make herself known to Jack.

But, even after she had said all that, she knew in her own mind that she would be sure to let Jack know at last, for she would never realize a moment's happiness until she was once more what she had been to Jack in the past.

It had been such a slight affair that had parted them, and that had drifted two hearts asunder.

Alas! how light a cause may moveDissensions between hearts that love—Hearts that the world in vain had tried,And sorrow but more closely tied;That stood the storm when waves were rough,Yet in a sunny hour fell off,Like ships that have gone down at seaWhen heaven was all tranquillity."

Chapter XXXIV.

During the week that followed, the words that Dorothy had heard in her dream constantly recurred to her.

At first she fought against the feeling that seemed to be forced upon her.

She cried out to herself that Jessie must live; but with that thought always came the one that, if Jessie recovered, it would mean the downfall of all her own future happiness.

At last her growing love for Jack Garner conquered her. She yielded to it. It was like the intoxication of rare wine, of sweet, subtle perfume, until at last, in secret, she confessed to herself that she loved him. She thought of nothing but that she loved Jack with all the strength and fervor of her despairing soul, and the only barrier between them was—Jessie.

To make matters all the worse, the sick girl made a confidante of her, and would talk to her for long hours at a time over her approaching marriage—that is, if she should recover.

Every word she said was like the sharp thrust of a sword to Dorothy; but day by day Dorothy could not help but notice the terrible change that was taking place in Jessie Staples.

Every afternoon her couch was drawn to the bay-window. She liked to be propped up where she could look out into the sunlit garden, with its green foliage and bright-hued flowers; for it was in the garden that Jack could be seen, pacing up and down under the trees, smoking his afternoon cigar.

She would always call for Jack when she saw him, and when he came into the room she would hold out her arms to him with a strange, low cry.

He would always kneel down by her side, talk to her, try to cheer her. Sleep would never come to her unless he sat by her side, holding her hands in his.

It was with great relief that Mr. Garner heard at length that Doctor Crandall was so much better that he would visit Jessie the next afternoon.

When he came Doctor Kendal took him at once to the sick-room, and there they held a long and secret consultation.

"I am obliged to say, sir, that I shall have to abandon the case," said Kendal. "I am completely dumbfounded with it. I have most carefully followed out your every suggestion, and yet the patient fails rapidly before my eyes day after day."

Doctor Crandall looked thoughtful.

When he left Jessie's couch he found Mr. Garner awaiting him in the library.

"What do you think of her, sir?" he asked, quickly.

"There is not much the matter," he replied; "a good tonic, rest, and a little cheerful society will soon set the young lady right again."

"It is the first time that you have seen her, doctor," said Jack, rather dubiously. "You never saw her in health, sir. You do not know how alarmingly she has changed for the worse. She had a brilliant color, but it has all gone."

"It will soon return," said the doctor, encouragingly; and with a few further words he left Jack, more mystified than ever.

For forty odd years he had enjoyed a large practice, but in all that time he had never had a case exactly like this.

He made up his mind then and there that there was something about this case which was beyond him—there was something about it that he could not fathom, that was shrouded in mystery.

He wired without delay, an urgent message to an eminent physician with whom he was on excellent terms. It was almost midnight when Doctor Schimpf arrived at the Garner mansion.

His friend, Doctor Crandall, was awaiting him, and together they made their way at once to the sick-room.

"This is an urgent case, I suppose," said Doctor Schimpf.

"I am afraid so," was the reply. "You will be able to judge when you see the patient."

Doctor Schimpf's stern face grew sterner still as he made his examination of poor Jessie. Then the doctors quitted the room and commenced their consultation.

Nadine Holt looked after them with a strange smile on her face, her black eyes glittering.

"Well," said Doctor Crandall, "I wonder if we both have the same opinion in regard to this case."

"It can admit of but one," returned Doctor Schimpf, with a shake of his head.

"And that is?"

"It is a case of slow poisoning," was the answer.

Doctor Crandall grasped his friend's hand.

"That was my view exactly," he said, huskily.

"There is but one way to proceed," returned Doctor Schimpf: "we must set a watch upon the inmates of the sick-room, and discover who is the perpetrator of this awful crime; and in the meantime make minute inquiries if there is any one under this roof who would be likely to be benefited by this poor girl's death. I propose that we proceed without an hour's delay."

"Agreed!" returned the other, promptly. "And I would suggest, as well, that a woman be secured, if possible, to undertake this task of ferreting out who is responsible for this awful crime that will soon terminate fatally if not nipped in the bud."

The next morning a young colored girl duly presented herself at the Garner mansion.

"I have brought you an assistant," said Doctor Crandall, leading her into the presence of Dorothy and Nadine Holt, and bowing to each in turn. "She is to obey your orders implicitly, and wait upon you. The medicines we have left are of an extremely pungent odor, and likely to overcome a person unused to them. She can attend to mixing the preparations for you, if you both consider her competent to do so, which you can tell after a short trial;" adding, besides: "One drop of this stains the hands, and it can not be got off for months. I thought this might be sufficient reason for placing this young girl at your disposal."

"You are very thoughtful, sir," said Nadine Holt, sweetly; but Dorothy spoke never a word.

Both doctors turned and looked keenly at her; then the conversation drifted quickly into another channel; but both had made up their minds that this boded no good for the slender, dark-looking woman with the blue glasses who hovered continually about the sick girl's couch.

As the doctors were leaving, under guise of giving a few words of instruction to Myra, the mulatto girl, they whispered hurriedly in her ear.

"I understand," she answered, with a nod of her head. "Nothing shall escape my eye."

The next day Doctor Crandall made minute inquiries regarding every member of the household, and every addition that had been made to it for the past few months; and he learned, casually, that the only person under that roof with whose history the Garners were not thoroughly acquainted was—Mrs. Brown.

Furthermore, he discovered that she had secured the place without proper recommendations. This he considered a serious affair. He was quite willing to give her the benefit of a doubt; still, it was too grave a matter of which he had charge. Every moment of time wasted in discovering the perpetrator of the awful crime was dangerous to Miss Staples, his beautiful patient, exposed to such deadly peril.

All unmindful of the espionage placed upon her, Dorothy went about her duties in the same faithful manner.

In the morning she read to and amused old Mrs. Garner. In the afternoon she attended to all the duties of the household; for in the midst of their difficulties their housekeeper had left them.

In the evening she relieved Nadine Holt from her arduous duties in the sick-room.

The only gleam of brightness that fell athwart her path was meeting Jack Garner at the table three times a day. Her life merged into one great longing to be near him.

She tried to picture how it would be when Jessie recovered and he should marry her. Of course, they would still dwell beneath that roof. Could the same home that held them hold her?

She could not endure seeing them so happy in each other's love. Whenever Jack entered the sick-room, Dorothy always made some pretense to leave it.

The sight of him bringing a flower to Jessie would be enough to almost break her heart with poignant grief.

She could not help but notice how handsome he was growing day by day.

Oh, what would she not have given for just one of the kindly words he used to speak to her, a tender look, a caress!

Chapter XXXV.

Not one thought did Dorothy give to Harry Kendal during these days. It is strange what a power some young girls possess in throwing off all tender thoughts from their hearts when the object of them has proven himself unworthy.

All love for Harry Kendal had gone out of her heart when she saw him choose Iris' society instead of her own, and she at the time his betrothed bride.

Dorothy's only hope was that Kendal would not penetrate her disguise, and never know what had become of her.

She did not know but what he was now betrothed to Iris, and *she did not care*. She was glad to be rid of him at any cost. She only wished that Nadine Holt—who was still so insanely in love with her false lover—knew how treacherous he was. She wished she dare tell her about Iris.

In her hours of loneliness little Pearl was a great comfort to Dorothy. She almost lost sight of her troubles at times in taking care of the child, who was quite as desolate in the world as herself.

She never forgot one morning that broke sunny enough for her, but ended in desolation more bitter to endure than death.

Mrs. Garner and herself were seated at the breakfast table, when Jack entered and took his seat opposite Dorothy. He bent his fair, handsome head, and kissed his mother as he passed her, and bowed courteously to "Mrs. Brown."

Both noticed that his fair, handsome face was very pale, and his right hand looked bruised. Mrs. Garner spoke of it at once.

"What is the matter—what has happened, Jack, my boy?" she asked, earnestly. "What does your agitation mean? You must tell me at once. Your—your appearance alarms me more than I can tell you."

He tried to laugh the matter off, but his mother would not be persuaded to change the subject.

"Well, then, if you *must* know, I will tell you when—we—are—alone," he said, a little unsteadily.

"You need not mind Mrs. Brown," she answered, quickly. "I do not hesitate speaking before her on any topic."

Dorothy rose hurriedly to her feet.

"I—I have finished my breakfast," she said, in the low tone she had assumed, and which so charmed every one; "and if you will excuse me, I shall be grateful."

Jack bowed courteously; but Mrs. Garner held out a fluttering hand to stay her steps.

"Do not go very far, Mrs. Brown," she said. "I may need you at any moment. Step into the conservatory and wait for further orders there."

With a bow of assent Dorothy glided from the room. She was sorry that Mrs. Garner had requested her to remain in the conservatory, for she knew full well that more or less of the conversation between mother and son must needs reach her ears.

The door had no sooner closed behind the slim, retreating figure ere Mrs. Garner turned quickly to her son, who was now pacing up and down the breakfast-room, with his arms folded tightly over his breast, his head crested proudly erect and a strange look in his eyes.

"Well, Jack." she said, at length, seeing that he was in no hurry to break the silence, "what is the matter? You used to tell your mother all your troubles when you were a little boy. Come to me with them now. Something has happened to disturb you greatly. I can see it in your face. Tell me what it is, my boy. Tell your mother what annoys you, my dear."

"You are right, mother; something *has* happened to disturb me," he said. "I ought not to worry you with it, but if you care to hear it you shall know all. You remember a conversation we had several months ago about—about little Dorothy, mother?"

"We *did* have a conversation about that girl, but I do not remember specially all that was said."

"You remember that I told you then, mother, that—that I still loved Dorothy, and if I ever came across the man who lured her away from me it would go hard with him or with me."

"I was in hopes that you were getting over that nonsense," she said, "especially since your betrothal to poor Jessie."

"I told you then, as I tell you now, mother, that I shall never forget Dorothy nor cease to love her. But for the story I have to tell: An hour since, as I was taking an early morning stroll to get a cigar, a little incident happened which caused me to pause and to quite forget my errand. It was only a little lame boy singing for pennies on the street, and the song that he sang touched my heart, as it has not been touched for long months, and thrilled every fiber of my being with a sharp, keen pain.

"You have heard the same song, mother. You remember how I rose and abruptly left the room when some young girl commenced to sing it in our drawing-room only a few short weeks ago. To-day I listened to it, spellbound; and the boy's accompaniment on the violin held me as one fascinated. I tried to move away, but could not, as you can judge by what occurred afterward. There was a strange fate in my standing there.

"I stood quite still and listened to the well-remembered words which carried me back so forcibly to my own past with Dorothy:

"'Far away in summer meadows,Where the merry sunbeams played,Oft I lingered 'mid the cloverSinging to a village maid.She was fairer than the fairest,Ever faithful, fond and true,And she wore beneath her bonnetAmber tresses tied with blue.

"'Ere the summer days departed,We had made a solemn vow,And I never, never weariedKissing her sweet cheek and brow.She was dearer than the dearest,Pure as drops of morning dew,And adown her back were hanging,Amber tresses tied with blue.

"'"Twas decreed that fate should part usEre the leaves of autumn fell,And two loving hearts were severed,That had loved each other well.She was all I had to cherish,We have bade our last adieu.Still I see in every visionAmber tresses tied with blue.'

Just at that moment a step sounded on the pavement.

"A man rushed down, hatless, from an adjacent mansion, and in a twinkling seized the offending young musician by the throat, and hurled him from the sidewalk, crying, fiercely:

"'I will teach you to come here every morning and to sing that accursed song of all others in front of my door. I have ordered you away twice before. I'll teach you better than to come back again.'

"The unprovoked assault upon the helpless cripple awoke all the anger in my nature.

"I sprang forward and separated them; but when I saw who the cripple's assailant was, my amazement knew no bounds.

"It was the young doctor who comes here to attend Jessie.

"He turned on me with terrible ferocity; then I recognized the fumes of wine on his breath.

"'This is the second time you have interfered in my business, Garner!' he cried, fairly foaming with rage. 'Once when you attempted to take Dorothy Glenn from me on the Staten Island boat, and—now.'

"I fell back as though he had struck me a terrible blow. In an instant I recognized him. I had been looking for him ever since Dorothy's flight. I had caught but a fleeting glimpse of him in the past, and his whiskers made such a change in him, no wonder I did not recognize him as he crossed our threshold; and this accounted for the manner in which he had managed to avoid me in my own household.

"'You! You fiend incarnate, have I found you at last? I could kill you here and now!' I cried as my fingers tightened around his throat. 'But I will give you one chance to save yourself. Name your own place as to where you will meet me. I did not recognize you before. You shall tell me what you have done with Dorothy Glenn, or I will kill you!'

"Those words seemed to recall him to his senses. He drew back defiantly, and his flashing black eyes met mine, while a terrible sneer curled his lips.

"'You shall never know whether Dorothy Glenn is living or dead!' he cried.

"I could have borne anything better than those scathing words from the lips of the man who had taken from me the girl I loved.

"'You will find me at my home up to the hour of noon,' he said. 'Make any arrangements you deem necessary.'

"I turned on my heel and left him; and here I am, awaiting a summons from him."

Mrs. Garner had risen slowly to her feet. The import of his words had just begun to dawn upon her.

"Jack!" she cried, wildly, throwing herself upon her knees at his feet, "is it to be a duel? Oh, my God, Jack, answer me!"

They heard a crash in the conservatory, but both were too excited to mind it.

"Let me go in your place," cried a hoarse voice from the doorway of the conservatory. "Pardon me, but I could not help overhearing all;" and Mrs. Brown advanced excitedly into the breakfast-room, and up to Jack's side. "Let me go in your place," she repeated. "Let me give my life for yours. I— I have nothing left to live for; you have."

Jack was deeply touched.

"You forget your little child," he said, gently. "Besides, any man might reasonably take up the quarrel of a lady, and, if need be, die in her defense, be she friend or stranger; but no woman should make such a sacrifice for a man. I thank you for the kindness of heart that prompted the words; but it can not be. I am sorry that you overheard my words to my mother. See! she has swooned away. I beg that you will take care of her, and let none of the household know what is about to occur."

As Jack Garner uttered the words, he kissed the prostrate form of his mother, and, turning, walked hastily out of the room.

Chapter XXXVI.

Dorothy then set about restoring Jack's mother, and with the first breath of returning consciousness she fled from the room and up to her own.

She was just about to seize her hat and cloak, and to dash out into the street, in the mad hope of overtaking him, all heedless of little Pearl's cry, as she woke from her sleep and held out her hand, when there came a sudden knock upon the door.

It was the colored maid.

"If you please, ma'am, you are wanted in Miss Staples' room."

"I—I can not go now," cried Dorothy, incoherently. "I have an urgent errand that I must attend to at once."

"But you must come, madame," said the girl, slowly, but very impressively.

"It is impossible," returned Dorothy, attempting to pass her by. "Every moment of my time is precious."

"But madame must go to the sick-room," reiterated the girl so earnestly that Dorothy paused.

"I will look in at the sick-room one moment," she said. "Then you—you must not detain me."

Suddenly she turned and asked:

"Do you know whether Mr. Garner is in the house?"

"He is in the library, ma'am."

"You are sure?" gasped Dorothy.

"Quite sure, ma'am. He also has had a message to come to the sick-room. I stopped and gave it to him myself on my way here."

Thus assured that he had not yet left the house, Dorothy breathed a great sigh of intense relief.

"I—I do not mind going to the sick-room with you now," she whispered, in a low, unsteady voice; and, all unconscious of what was to accrue from it, Dorothy followed her companion from the room and up to Jessie's chamber.

The silence of death was upon all things as she parted the silken *portières* and entered the room where the sick girl lay, white and gasping, upon the couch.

The two doctors made way for her, motioning her to advance to the couch.

"Oh! she is not dying—not dying?" gasped Dorothy, with a wild wail of terror. "You must not tell me that!"

"Are you so very much surprised?" asked Doctor Crandall, slowly and impressively.

"Oh, she must not die—-she must not die!" she cried. "Where is all your vaunted skill if you can not save her life?"

"Man can work against the skill of man," significantly replied Doctor Crandall, "but not against the will of Heaven."

"But is she dying?" wailed Dorothy, grasping the ice-cold hands.

"She shall not die if we can save her," simultaneously echoed both doctors.

They uttered the words in so strange a tone that Dorothy turned and looked at them in wonder.

At that moment Mr. Garner entered the room. His face was still very pale, but he was outwardly calm.

He was just in time to catch the last words, and he stepped up hurriedly to the doctor ere he could utter another word to Dorothy.

"Do you say that my betrothed is dying?" he cried, hoarsely, flinging himself on his knees beside the couch, on the side opposite to where Dorothy was.

"What we have to say had better be deferred for a few moments, until he is more calm and better able to bear the shock," said Doctor Schimpf, nodding in the direction where Mr. Garner knelt prostrated with grief.

Dorothy had become strangely calm, and both doctors noticed that she intently watched the actions of young Mr. Garner.

"I think I have unearthed the secret of the whole affair," whispered Doctor Crandall to his friend. "Watch the gaze Mrs. Brown is bending upon the betrothed lover of the girl who lies sick unto death!"

He motioned the doctor back into the recess of the bay-window.

"Let me finish my story here," he whispered under his breath. "This is what I would say: This strange woman in the black dress loves Mr. Garner. Ah! you start, my friend. So did I when the thought first flashed across my mind. Within the last few moments this thought has settled into a conviction. She is the only one interested in the death of Miss Staples. Look carefully into the chain of evidence I present to you, and you will have the same opinion that I have formed, no doubt.

"In the first place, as we both know, Miss Staples' sudden attack of illness dated from a few days after this mysterious young woman crossed this threshold.

"Who she is, or whence she came, no one seems to have been clever enough to find out.

"She has come and gone from this house, alone, and at all hours, no one questioning her movements.

"She has taken full charge of the patient, from midnight until early morning, and each forenoon our patient seems to have grown alarmingly worse. We have both discovered the presence of arsenic, which has been administered to her.

"And now last, but by no means least, I have been observing this mysterious woman with keen scrutiny. I could stake my life upon it she wears a wig, that her complexion is a 'made-up' one. By this you will understand me to say that the lines we see traced upon her face are the work of art, not time. The eyes covered by those blue glasses are bright as stars. In short, she is not the middle-aged personage that she appears, but is a young woman, or rather a fiend incarnate, in disguise.

"I propose within the next few moments to lay the matter before Mr. Garner, and to gain his sanction to compel her to throw off this disguise before she leaves this room, to confront her with the evidence of her crime, and to force her to make a full confession at the bedside of her would-be victim."

"I quite agree with your plan," assented the other. "But there is one precaution which we must not forget: the key must be turned in the lock and removed, if you would have your bird securely caged. Delays are dangerous. Let Mr. Garner be told the terrible truth without a moment's delay, and we will rest the case wholly with him."

Without attracting attention, Doctor Crandall called Mr. Garner into the recess of the bay-window, while Doctor Schimpf engaged Dorothy in conversation to pass the time away.

To attempt to describe Jack Garner's astonishment, which gradually deepened into the most intense horror as the terrible story was unfolded to him, can better be imagined than described.

"Jessie suffering from the effects of poison?" he gasped, incredulously. "Great Heaven! how can I believe such an uncanny tale? Miss Staples has not an enemy in the whole world, I am sure. No one could have a motive in attempting to put her out of the way."

"Will you answer one question?" said the doctor, looking earnestly at the young man.

"Anything which you may ask," quickly returned the other.

"Did you ever have any other sweetheart than Miss Staples? Did any other woman ever love you in the past?"

For a moment Jack hesitated, and his fair, handsome face flushed; then he frankly raised his eyes and met the keen gaze fixed upon him.

"I have no hesitancy in acknowledging that I did have a romance in my life before my betrothal to poor Jessie. But she knew about it from beginning to end."

"Did you give this girl up for Miss Staples? Pardon me for asking such a direct question, but your answer is vitally important."

The handsome face into which the old doctor gazed grew very white, and the lines about the firm mouth deepened into an expression of pain.

"My little sweetheart disappeared one day with a handsomer man than I," he said, huskily, "and from that time to this I have never looked upon her false but fair face."

"Did she love you in those days?" was the next query.

"I wonder that you can ask the question," said Jack, with a touch of haughty bitterness. "Does it look very much as though she loved me when she ran away with another man? On the contrary, any one could see that, in pursuing the course she did toward me, she must have detested me. I never saw this Mrs. Brown before we engaged her as a companion to my mother, nor has Jessie, I am sure. I am completely at sea," Jack added, "and therefore I leave the matter entirely with you. If Jessie is dying of slow poison, I beseech you to discover the perpetrator of the deed, at any cost— aye, and though it takes every dollar of my fortune, the wretch shall be punished to the full extent of the law."

Chapter XXXVII.

Quietly the doctors filed into the room, and one of them turned the key in the door.

It was Dr. Crandall who undertook the delicate task of unmasking the suspected would-be murderess.

"I will tell you," he said, slowly. "The poor girl on the couch beside which you have often knelt is dying of slow poison, administered to her by some person beneath this roof."

Dorothy sprang from her chair and reeled backward, looking at him with widely dilated eyes. She never knew how it happened, but in that instant of time a terrible thought came to her. Could Jack Garner be guilty of administering it to her, to free himself from the bonds he so cruelly hated?

Oh, God! how the thought tortured her. She would not—she could not believe it.

"Some one under this roof has been guilty of this most atrocious act," continued the doctor, in a stern voice. "We suspect—we know the guilty party, and that party is in this very room!"

Dorothy clasped her hands in dumb agony, and her terrified eyes never left the form of him who had once been her lover.

"You do not answer me, Mrs. Brown," said the doctor, frowning. "What have you to say?"

"What could I say?" she sobbed, piteously.

"The one who is guilty of this diabolical deed must be held accountable for it," said the doctor, facing her sternly. "A just punishment must and shall be meted out to the wicked party. If you say that you will not admit the truth, then I will turn the affair over to Mr. Garner, here and now!"

What would they do with Jack? In imagination she saw him in a prison cell, perhaps doomed to drag out all the after years of his life there, and the thought seemed to drive her to madness.

"I will take it upon myself, and Jack shall go free," she said to herself—"yes blameless and free."

Slowly the doctor stepped around to Jack's side.

"What have you to say in this matter, Mr. Garner?" he said.

"Let me answer instead of him," Dorothy panted, hoarsely. "He knows nothing about it. Oh, hear me!—listen to me, I pray you! It is I—I whom you must hold guilty. Do with me as you will!"

Both of the doctors nodded toward each other. A groan broke from Garner's lips—this acknowledgement was so terrible for him to hear from this strange woman's lips.

"Who are you, and what was your motive for this horrible crime?" asked the doctor, sternly. "You must make a clean breast of why you attempted to poison Miss Staples, here and now."

There was one person in that room who listened to Dorothy's most extraordinary confession, white with terror, and that was—Nadine Holt.

She knew full well that the stranger was entirely guiltless; then why under heaven had she placed herself in such a horrible position?

Nadine recovered her outward composure by a great effort, and listened intently to what they were saying.

"You must reveal your identity here and now," Doctor Crandall was repeating, vehemently, "or I shall force you to do so. When we once become convinced who you are, and your motive for this crime, then we will know how to proceed against you. In the first place, I order you to remove both the wig and glasses which we have discovered that you are wearing. Your identity is the first step in this matter."

Like a flash Dorothy flung herself at Jack Garner's feet.

Ere he could put out his hand toward her, Doctor Crandall had sprung forward, and with a quick motion gently but deftly snatched the wig from her head and the glasses from her eyes, and Dorothy—Dorothy Glenn stood revealed, in all her terror, before the astonished gaze of Jack Garner and Nadine Holt.

"You—you!" cried Jack, in horror too great for words.

"Save me—save me!" gasped the girl.

He wondered that he did not go mad, then and there at the sight of her.

"Let me go!" she panted, imploring.

The doctor shook his head.

"You must be held answerable for your crime," he said, sternly. "You showed no pity to the girl lying here so helpless, and why should it be shown you? She lies here in a deep sleep, and when she awakens we shall know whether it is life or death she has to face. We hope it is life, but we can not be too sure. In the interim, while we decide your fate, you should thank Heaven that your plans are frustrated. We can not decide, until the crisis is past, as to what is best to be done."

"Jack," she whispered again, "let me go far away and leave you with Jessie. She will recover, and you will marry her and be happy after all, and I—I will never cross your path again."

He tore away the white little hands that clung to him, and turned to the doctors. They were awed at the sight of his white, desperate face.

"You have both assured me that Miss Staples will not die from this poisoning," he said, hoarsely; "and I—I, the one most vitally interested in this affair, say to you: Open that door and let her go her way."

Ah, God! that they should meet and part like this, after all those weary months of heartache!

"God only knows her object in coming here in disguise and committing this awful crime," was his mental thought; but aloud, he only said:

"Go, and may Heaven forgive you! Go to the father of your child."

A terrible lump rose in his throat; he could say no more.

The little one had crept out of Dorothy's arms, and out into the middle of the floor; but Dorothy never, in that awful moment, thought of the child. She was so stunned that the full import of his words did not strike her just then.

She only knew that he was opening the door for her, and harshly commanding her to go.

Like a storm-driven swallow, with one quick glance in his face, the girl turned and fled from the room, and out of the house.

"You were too generous toward her," cried one of the doctors. "See! she has abandoned her little child, Mr. Garner."

Then suddenly the doctor stopped short, and looked first at the fair-haired, beautiful babe, then at Mr. Garner, and said no more.

Chapter XXXVIII.

When Dorothy fled so precipitately from the room, she fairly ran into the arms of a man who was crouching at one side, listening intently. With a muttered imprecation, he drew back, and it was then Dorothy saw his face.

"Hush! On your life, don't dare to make an outcry!" cried the harsh voice of Harry Kendal.

Before she could utter the scream that welled up from her heart, he had seized her in his strong arms, thrown a dark shawl over her head, dashed out into the street with her, and into a cab in waiting.

Too weak to struggle, too weak to cry out, her head fell backward upon her abductor's shoulder, and she knew no more.

When she awoke to consciousness of what was transpiring about her, she found herself still in the coach beside Kendal, and the vehicle was whirling along through the sunshine and shadow of a country road with alarming rapidity.

"Dorothy—my darling Dorothy!" he cried, clasping her hands and showering kisses upon her upturned face. "Oh, Dorothy, my little bride that is to be, why did you fly from me so cruelly the morning after the great ball at our home in Yonkers?"

"Do not speak to me! Stop this coach immediately, and let me get out!" she cried. "How dare you attempt to thrust your unwelcome face in my way again? Go back to Iris Vincent, for whom you left me; or to Nadine Holt, whose heart and whose life you have wrecked. I know you for what you are, and I abhor you a thousand times more than I ever imagined I fancied you."

"Do you mean that you do not wish to go back to the Yonkers home and marry me?" he demanded.

But before she could find time to reply, he went on:

"You were terribly foolish to grow so jealous of Iris Vincent as to run away from me. Why, I—I was merely flirting with her because she was pretty.

"Why, she is married now, and at the other end of the world, for aught I know or care. I can only add that, from the moment I learned of your disappearance, I have been searching for you night and day. Oh, Dorothy, now that I have found you, do not treat me like this, I beseech you! Let us kiss and make up. We are driving direct toward the parsonage, where we are to be married.

"Few men would care for you so much upon making the terrible discovery that you had fled from home and directly to the arms of an old lover, remaining under his roof until you were cast out from it by that lover himself. I do not know even what your quarrel with him was about. I do not ask to know. The object which took me there, I do not mind telling you. I had a quarrel with your lover, Jack Garner. We were to meet early this morning to settle the affair of honor; but as he did not show up to make the arrangements, I forced my way into his house, in order that I might not miss him. I heard him turning you from his door. Then amazement held me spell-bound. I shall take this into account when—when I have my settlement with him, later on. Any indignity offered to you shall be my affair, as your husband, to settle."

Dorothy had drawn back from him listening with horror to the words that fell from his lips.

"The duel must be averted at any cost," she told herself; yet she could not—oh, she could not!—marry him. "I must think of some way out of this," thought Dorothy, in the wildest agony. "I must save myself, and save him, too."

But in a moment, while she was pondering over the affair, the vehicle came to a sudden stop, and, looking out, she saw it was standing before the wide entrance-gate of a parsonage.

"Here we are!" cried Kendal, holding out his hand to her.

"I have not said that I would marry you," she cried. "How dared you bring me here?"

"That fact was settled between you and me so long ago that you surprise me by your words," he said, angrily.

"There is such a thing as a person changing her mind," said Dorothy, as she leaped from the carriage, and stood facing him under the trees.

"Surely you do not mean that you have changed yours?" retorted Kendal, knowing that his best policy was to temporize with her.

"I have, indeed," declared the girl; "and you will therefore oblige me, Mr. Kendal, by re-entering your carriage and driving along."

"Do you think I would leave you here, Dorothy," he said, in his most winning voice—"here, at this strange parsonage? I should say not! If you object to marrying me now, I know it is only through pique; but still I say that I shall await your own good time; and, as the song goes, 'When love has conquered pride and anger, you will call me back again.' Do get in, Dorothy, darling; do not make a scene here. See! they are watching us from the window. Get in, and we will drive on to Yonkers. It is only four miles farther up the road. I promise you you shall have your own way. Mrs. Kemp is at the old home. You will be welcomed with open arms."

"Take your hand off my arm, or I shall scream!" cried the girl, struggling to free herself.

Quick as a flash he seized her, and, with the rapidity of lightning, thrust her back into the coach.

"Drive on—drive on!" Kendal yelled to the driver—"you know where!" and despite Dorothy's wild, piercing cries, the coach fairly flew down the white, winding road, and was soon lost to view amid the dense trees.

It soon became evident to Dorothy that she was only losing her strength in shouting for help.

Kendal was leaning back in his seat, with the most mocking smile on his lips that ever was seen.

"It is a pity to waste so much breath on the desert air," he sneered. "I would advise you to stop before you become exhausted, as there is no one to hear you and to come to your aid."

But Dorothy did not heed, and renewed her cries the more vociferously.

He had said thoughtlessly, that her cries would startle the horses, never dreaming that this would indeed be the case. But, much to his alarm, he noticed that their speed was increasing with every instant of time. It broke upon him all too soon that they were indeed running away, and that the driver was powerless to check them.

In great alarm, Kendal sprang to his feet and threw open the door. That action was fatal; for at that instant the horses suddenly swerved to the right, and he was flung head foremost from the vehicle; the wheels passed over him, and the next instant the coach collided with a large tree by the roadside, and Dorothy knew no more.

Up this lonely path walked a woman, young and very fair, but with a face white as it would ever be in death. And as her despairing eyes traveled up and down the scene they suddenly encountered the white upturned face of a woman lying in the long grass.

With a great cry she reached her side.

"Dead!" she whispered in a voice of horror, as she knelt beside the figure lying there, and placed her hand over her heart. But no; the heart beneath her light touch beat ever so faintly. "Thank God! this poor creature is not dead," murmured the stranger, fervently.

Chapter XXXIX.

Dorothy opened her eyes wide, looking up in wonder at the pale, sweet face bending over her.

"Poor child!" murmured a sweet, pathetic voice.

A kindly hand raised her, gently but firmly, from the dew-wet grass, and pushed the damp, golden curls back from her face.

The caressing touch thrilled the girl's being through every fiber.

"You ask why I am here!" she sobbed. "Let me tell you: I came here to die. Death would have come to me, I feel sure, if you had not crossed my path. I should have crept to the brink of the bank yonder, and thrown myself down into the river, and ended a life that is not worth the living."

"You must have seen a great deal of trouble to cause you to talk like that."

"I have seen more trouble than any other person on earth," retorted Dorothy, bitterly.

"Have you lost friends, or those nearer and dearer to you?" came the gentle question, and Dorothy did not hesitate, strangely enough, to answer it.

"I never had a relative that I can remember," she answered, with a little sob. "But I have lost my lover—my lover! He is to wed another, and that other a girl who was once my dearest friend."

"Your story is a sad one," replied the stranger, soothingly; "but it might have been worse—much worse. What if you had lost a husband whom you loved, or a little child whom you idolized? That would have been trouble before which such as you are grieving over now would have paled as the stars pale before a strong noon-day sun.

"I do not ask you your story, my poor girl, but listen, and I will tell you mine, and you can then judge how much mightier is my grief than yours."

"If you look through the trees yonder you will see a great stone mansion on the brow of the hill.

"It is my home. I live there with a dear young husband who adores me; my slightest wish is his law.

"I have liveried servants who anticipate and execute my slightest wish. I have all that wealth can buy and love can lavish upon me, but, God help me! I am the most unhappy creature that walks this flower-strewn earth.

"I have endured a sorrow so great that the wonder is it has not turned my brain. Some few months since I was happy in the love of a little child. Oh! I idolized my babe with a love that seemed greater than human affection. It was the loadstar of my life.

"'Take care! Beware!' cried one and all. 'Such idolatry is not wise; it displeases Heaven.'

"I laughed, and did not heed. One day we discharged a worthless servant and he cried out to my husband, as he turned away from the door: 'You shall repent this! I will yet wring the heart of you and yours to the very core; and in that moment, remember me!'

"A week passed. One night I suddenly awoke from a troubled dream about my babe.

"I put out my hand. It was not in its little crib of white and gold. I sprang from my couch with wild cries that alarmed the household, for I could not find my child. She was gone, as if the earth had opened and swallowed her. But on the pillow of the crib the servants found a note which bore these words:

"'My revenge is complete. It is useless to search for your child, for by the time this meets your eye your little one will have found a watery grave.'

"I was wild with grief for days and weeks. And when I became somewhat rational, and could understand what was passing about me, I learned the terrible truth—the sad, pitiful story: my babe had indeed found a watery grave. They found a little shoe, its cape, and portions of its dress floating on the waves the next morning. But the body was never recovered; it had drifted out to sea. Now you will not wonder why I wander up and down this lonely path at midnight—why I listen on my bended knees for hours to the whispering voice of the waves. It seems to me like the voice of my little child; and some day I shall follow her into the dark, cold waves, and be at rest with my darling whose tiny hands beckon me down to death in the cold, watery depths whose waves are glinted by the golden light of the flickering stars."

Dorothy scarcely breathed, so intense was her effort to restrain herself until the other had finished.

In fewer words than we can explain it she had flung her arms about the stranger's neck and breathed out to her the startling story of that never-to-be-forgotten night when she had rescued from the waves the child this poor young mother was describing.

"Oh, take me to my child!" she cried. "Now—now! Let not an instant's time elapse. Every moment is precious. I can not wait—I can not!"

Then Dorothy had her own story to tell: that she dared not return to Jack Garner's home, where she had left little Pearl; and she told her the whole story from beginning to end. Then came another revelation:

"Jack Garner is my husband's partner!" the strange lady cried. "Come back with me, and leave it to me to fully establish your innocence of the atrocious crime of which they believe you guilty.

"We have never visited at each other's homes, strangely enough, because of some slight disagreement in the firm at the very time Mr. Garner was taken in.

"Come and talk it over with my husband. We will do whatever he decides."

Oh, the great rejoicing in the old stone mansion! The horses were hitched up without an instant's delay, and driven like mad into the city, arriving at the Garner mansion just as the clock was striking twelve.

The old servant who answered the loud peal of the bell was shocked at the sight of the beautiful lady who rushed past him in the corridor, crying out: "Oh, for the love of Heaven, bring quickly to me the baby whom you call Pearl!"

Dorothy and the lady's husband followed.

The great disturbance awoke Jack Garner. He heard the scurrying of feet past his door. They stopped at the next room, where the little abandoned babe was sleeping.

The next instant a great, wild, happy cry rent the air, which the angels must have heard and wept rejoicingly over; and he heard the joyful cry:

"Yes; it is my child—my own little, lost child!"

Robing himself hurriedly, Jack quickly opened the door; but his partner was standing there, and thrust him back.

Jack knew of the loss of the little one, and his partner explained to him how mysteriously it had been found, and by Jack's old sweetheart, Dorothy Glenn.

"Then the child she had here was not her own?" cried Jack, white as death.

And as the whole story began to dawn upon him, Jack buried his fair, handsome, haggard face in his hands, and wept for joy.

But when his partner touched upon the subject of Dorothy's being accused of poisoning Miss Staples, he sprang up hastily and grasped the other's hand.

"The accusation was not true," cried Jack. "Dorothy was not guilty. A girl whom Jessie had known for years, and who was at her bedside, did the deed. She wrote a full confession. I found it under my plate at the dinner-table. Nadine Holt has fled to escape just punishment. Oh, how I wish I could find poor, abused Dorothy, to tell her the truth!"

And when he found Dorothy was beneath that roof, and at Jessie Staples' bedside, his joy knew no bounds.

He sought her there at once to crave her pardon for the unjust suspicion, and no one ever knew just exactly what passed between the sick girl lying there, Dorothy, and her old lover.

In his great generous-heartedness, Jack sent hurriedly out to learn the fate of the hapless Kendal. He was not dead, they soon discovered, but in a very critical condition. And Jack's generosity went so far as to bring his rival beneath that roof, and nurse him back to health and strength.

From the first, even while lying on her sick-bed, Jessie took the greatest interest in the young doctor who, she remembered, had always been so kind to her; and as soon as she was able, she begged that her chair might be drawn up to his bedside, that she might show him her kindly sympathy. And in the days and weeks that they were thus thrown together, Jessie learned to care for the handsome, dark-eyed Harry Kendal quite as much as she had ever cared for Jack.

One day, when the sun was shining, and the birds were twittering to each other of early spring, Harry Kendal asked the pale, sweet girl who knelt beside his couch to be his bride.

And she answered him, through her bitter tears, that though she had been mad enough to learn to love him, it could never be, for she was betrothed to Jack.

Jack had entered the room unperceived by both, and had heard all, and with the magnanimity so characteristic of him, he stepped nobly forward and placed Jessie's hand in that of the man she loved.

"I absolve you from your promise, my dear girl," he said. "You must wed him whom you love best. Never mind me."

"But you?" sobbed Jessie. "I—I will accept my freedom only on one condition, Jack; and that is, that you ask Dorothy to fill my place—aye, to take her own old place again in your heart and life!"

"Not now," he said; "but perhaps I may speak to her some time in the future."

And he must have spoken to her, for three weeks later there was a double wedding at the Garner mansion; and there never were two more beautiful brides than Jessie and Dorothy, nor two happier young husbands than Harry Kendal and Jack Garner; and Jack never ceased blessing the fates that gave to him for his bride, after all his trials, pretty Madcap Dorothy. But, then, the course of true love never did ran smooth.

THE END.

Milton Keynes UK
Ingram Content Group UK Ltd.
UKHW050037220624
444555UK00004B/427